Rayyan Dabbous

SYRIANS FOR SALE

LEBANESE STYLE

This book is a work of fiction. The characters are all fictional; any similarities to them in real life are purely coincidental.

Fact, after all, is far crueler than fiction.

"All I want to say is that they don't really care about us." - Michael Jackson.

To Zorro (2011-2018)

Who, unlike some, aspired to be human

THE TRUTH ACCORDING

TO U.S. PRESIDENT RONALD CHUMP

Fake news.

Two words to sum up my testimony to you, Prime Minister Fakhouri. *Fake* news.

Ever since my arrival to Lebanon, a country as small as the state of Connecticut, I have been breathing the damp air of CNN-worthy lies brought with your Mediterranean waves. First of all, *where is Hezbollah?* I thought these guys were everywhere. All I found, as my private jet made its descent, was a beautiful sandy coastline with long stern palm trees and large fancy buildings. A nice touch, too, was the zigzagging of your street lights, some on, some off, across the main highway that travels along the shore. Impeccable show by your Ministry of Electricity for my grand arrival.

A show, of course, financed by American taxpayers' money. I assumed the billions of dollars we donate to nations like yours every year go to fighting ISIS, which must be sprouting with recruits in some Beiruti ghetto as we speak. *But where are they?* My convoy passed through much of Beirut's main attractions - the seashore with all those loaded tourists from the Gulf with their many wives and many children, the coastline that begins with the *American* University of Beirut and ends with the *American* chain of McDonalds, and here, downtown Beirut, which, with its high-rises, banks, and hotels, looks more like New York's Financial District than its Bronx.

That's why I will call you out, Mr. Prime Minister, whenever you complain about how Lebanon needs more and more money for its refugee population. In the past few weeks, your administration has caused the international community much stress and trouble with the ultimatum it has placed regarding its Syrian refugees, who are threatened to be forced back to Syria imminently.

Of course, I would have done the same thing if I had a million and a half Mexicans flocking into the US border all at once. But Mexico is not Syria, Mr. Fakhouri. What your administration wants to do is send back these people to a country at war - a bloody battle, which, because of *American national security*, may not end until all these jihadists are completely exterminated. Your threat to the UN members is therefore unwarranted - you should have dealt with the matter more intelligently, more astutely... more like how I do things myself.

The Canadian Prime Minister killed Mr. Saito, his Japanese counterpart? I don't believe it. In fact, I was hanging in his room yesterday morning, before we all convened to our first session at this emergency UN meeting in Star

Square's political compound. Since my suite is located at one end of the Corridor of Nations' East Hallway, and Mr. Judeaux's is adjacent to mine, a few feet into the corridor, I had to anyway pass by the Canadian Suite to use the elevator. Plus, I wanted to check out the measurements of his suite.

Why would I care about that? Don't get the wrong idea, buddy. I was not there to frame him. I don't care about Canada - it was *China's* suite, which was opposite of Mr. Judeaux's, that I wanted to know the size of. Trust me on this, the trade war I have recently threatened the international community with would have surely ensued if I realized that the President of *America* was carefully placed in the smallest room of the *East* Hallway as a conspiracy against the *West*.

If there was any crime the Canadian Prime Minister was trying not to commit that day - it was a fashion crime. While my eyes were scanning his suite inch-by-inch during our brief, somewhat awkward small-talk, Narcissus, at the other end of the room, could not take his eyes away from his own reflection. He was so preoccupied with his hair, brushing it, un-brushing it and brushing it again, that he would even take a pause every five seconds and move his chin sideways, as though to check the level with which his hair falls over his head.

That surely was the gravest of his concerns that morning. *A murderer?* No way. I can't see that dandy pretty boy getting his own manicured hands stained with blood. He would get daddy to do it for him.

Plus, why would he do it? He keeps bragging about how welcoming his country has been for Syrian refugees. His first speech during that morning session I mentioned was fueled with this arrogant attitude. As you saw, he was sandwiched, like the English Channel, between the British Prime Minister and the French President, and throughout his speech, he would turn right and left with the wheels of his swivel chair, as though his sweeping words must necessarily concern us all. *Global community... global citizens... global responsibility.* Bullshit. If he was twice the man of his words, he would pack all those Syrians back with him to Canada.

Wouldn't that worry me? I see what you're doing there, Mr. Fakhouri. I don't need to go big on Japan to ward off the threat of Syrians flocking into the US once they start claiming asylum from the brutality of Canadian weather. I was planning on extending the Great Wall of America to our northern borders, anyway.

Who do I suspect to be the murderer? The killer must be the head of the arguably weakest nation at this meeting, the Brazilian President, Ms. Vilma Yosef. I am still perplexed by the reason she voted *for* equally splitting the refugees between us fifteen countries. You've read the news, haven't you? Their crumbling economy cannot support a hundred thousand new *aliens*, spat out of nowhere! She must have joined the YES camp to blend in with them, as a disguise to her real agenda.

I saw her disgusted face every time that unsophisticated Australian Prime Minister, Ms. Jasmine David, smiled at her. Of course, I understand anyone's reaction upon seeing the gap between the Aussie's front teeth, which, given how she showed up in jeans to the meeting, must be as wide as the gap between our respective net worth. That said, the look Ms. Yosef gave her Australian counterpart - *and I spotted this within a split second* - was first oozing with bitterness and then followed with a cover-up smile. It's all a show. She hates Australia as much as Syria. Why else would she vote for the proposed motion? For the love of *humanity*?

Fake news. It's all fake bullshit news, Mr. Fakhouri. My word of advice to you in this quick, behind-the-doors investigation, is to be wary of kindness. My honest approach with the Syrian refugee crisis might make me a sheep in wolf's clothing, but some of the world leaders here, I guarantee, are wolves in sheep's clothing. The Victorian England Witch, the Serious Mercedes Autobot, the Know-it-All Voltaire - you must especially be cynical of *them*, no matter what loving words they tell you. Trust me, Mr. Prime Minister, not a single nation here wants your refugees. *Not one.* What would I do in your place? Lock everyone up.

THE TRUTH ACCORDING

TO BRAZIL PRESIDENT VILMA YOSEF

Why did I vote for the motion to split the refugees?

I see suspicion in your eyes, Prime Minister Fakhouri, and it infuriates me. Who had the audacity to accuse _me_ of murder, President Vilma Yosef, a lady of my esteem, with an ancestral nobility that stretches back to _Rei Dom José Primeiro_! Did this liar, whom I suspect to be that audacious German Chancellor Markella Angels, also, with her intimidating face, make you forget the deep roots Brasil shares with _Líbano_? Today, seven million Brazilians are originally from your small country. This means that, had they all retained their passports, the Lebanese

Parliament would meet in *Praça Estrela*, not Nejmeh Square, and you, Mr. Fakhouri, would be called Marcos.

I voted for the motion because large waves of immigration are common to Brazil. The Lebanese diaspora, for example, has also come in big batches... some after the Civil Strife of 1860... others after the Great Famine of 1915... and a lot more during the Civil War of 1975. Plus, Lebanese have been excellent businessmen, and I see no reason why Syrians can't also turn around their fortune with the blessing of *Nossa Senhora Aparecida*. Don't get me wrong... I am not saying that Lebanese and Syrians are the same.

Leave that for the stupid American *bufão*, Mr. Chump, who, throughout our first meeting yesterday, kept insisting that he had spotted flocks of loaded Arab tourists from the Gulf, with their many wives and many children, idly roaming around your coastline at night. When the baffled Swedish Prime Minister, Ms. Carolina

Springborg, assured him these families were actually poor and idle Syrian refugees with nowhere to hang around but the coastline, he would not listen.

My point, anyway, is that Brazil, no matter what the German Chancellor told you, is not shaken when it must welcome a large number of foreigners to its cities. The one exception, that said, would be the time we hosted not a flock of refugees but the World Cup. Another German conspiracy. *Don't you see the pattern, Mr. Fakhouri?* We lost to Germany seven to one in 2014, and today, one single vote is necessary to outnumber the seven nations that voted against the motion to split the refugees. *7-1, 1-7.* A code game engineered by Markella Angels.

Though political corruption is often unfairly seen as exclusive to Latin America, no one has ever questioned the long-standing tenure of this German Chancellor - a reign that started shortly after Brazil was crowned champion in FIFA 2002, which was co-hosted by Japan. *There's another pattern for you, Mr. Fakhouri.* Brazil screws Germany in a World Cup hosted by Japan. Almost two decades later, Germany screws Brazil in a World Meeting thanks to Japan. *Don't you see the psychological terror, the crazy codes and patterns?* Didn't the Germans after all come up with The Enigma?

Why then was I giving Ms. Jasmine David, the Australian Prime Minister, a nasty look? Is this what the all-seeing German spy informed you about? *Nossa Senhora!* Let me describe to you what this is all about. The moment you refer to happened yesterday when our conversation about Syrian refugees steered toward the topic of integrating Syrian women into the workforce of host countries. My gorgeous counterpart from Sweden - *linda maravilhosa*! - was explaining to the table her own country's success with Syrian refugee women, whose handicraft boosted the economy.

During Carolina Springborg's passionate explanation, I could not help but notice the unconvinced shrug Ms. David would make every fifteen seconds. *As though women could not be useful for society!* To make matters worse, when that womanizer American President interrupted Carolina's speech, more out of obsession with her beauty than her words, the Australian Prime Minister discreetly laughed at the *bufão's* sexist joke. This is why, Mr. Fakhouri, I could not but glare at this *traidora* of a woman.

The Japanese President chocked from a peanut allergy and his emergency shot was found in the Canadian Prime Minister's blazer pocket? Interesting. I must then bring up yesterday morning, when I went down to have breakfast before our meeting. I was waiting for the elevator and I could not help but hear whispers coming down the East Hallway. Discreetly, and forgive my prying, I glanced at the ajar door where the voices were coming from and I moved away from the elevator. I took a few steps toward the mirror by the Chinese President's suite, which was opposite the Canadian's, and pretended to be giving my hair a few more adjustments with my fingers.

What I found through the reflection was the handsome Canadian, who was also fixing his hair, and he was paying the least attention to the blabbering of what I believed was the voice of the US President. At that point, Mr. Judeaux was not wearing his blazer, which was hung on his brown coat rack a few feet from where President Chump must have been standing.

So do I think the US President did it? I do not believe my eye account that morning is this much significant to your investigation, Prime Minister Fakhouri - at least not nearly as significant as what I saw on the night of the crime. Earlier, you informed me that you found President Saito's emergency shot - *Nossa Senhora Aparecida rest his soul!* - inside Prime Minister Judeaux's blazer. What perplexes you about this fact, I believe, is the reason why the Canadian didn't get rid of that syringe as soon as he got his hands on it, rather than get caught with it afterward. I have the key to the mystery, Mr. Fakhouri.

To solve it, you must be aware of the German Chancellor's eccentric behavior yesterday. *Please bear with me.* I am not just saying this because I hold some historical grudge against the Germans - leave that argument when you interview the British Prime Minister or the French President. Anyway, you can ask the whole floor about Markella Angels' weird obsession ever since she arrived to this political compound. The German woman, for some reason, has elected herself, as with her Chancellorship, to the role of the concierge in the Corridor of Nations. In the morning, at noon, and at night - at any point of the day, you would constantly see her running around with garbage bags. South African

President Leymah Maseko and I even came up with a nickname for Markella: *Trashella*.

The reason for this behavior used to baffle me - but not anymore. *Listen to this, Mr. Fakhouri*. That night of the crime, when I was by the corridor fighting with President Chump, and you'll hear more about this later, I couldn't help but notice furtive movements coming from the East Hallway. People were coming and going, and for a long time, I could only spot their silhouettes. Let us remember that the East Hallway hosts the suites of USA, Canada and China by the left side of the elevator, and those of South Africa, Iran and Germany by the right side. None of the leaders of these countries were remotely close to the East Hallway that evening - except for two individuals, whom I finally spotted from the corner of my eyes.

You have to trust me on this, Mr. Fakhouri. It was the Canadian, who, according to you, needed to get rid of the syringe, and the German, who, according to me, loved getting personally rid of garbage. The former is naive and trusts everyone and the latter malicious and cannot be trusted. *What can I tell you, Mr. Fakhouri?* German spies were excellent double agents.

THE TRUTH ACCORDING

TO GERMANY CHANCELLOR MARKELLA

ANGELS

What was I doing with Prime Minister Judeaux during the night of the crime?

I am very happy you asked me this question, Mr. Fakhouri. _Fantastisch_. Where to start? When President Saito was taking his last breath, as you mention, at 7:45PM, at the step of his suite's door, I was indeed with my Canadian colleague running around the East Hallway. This was long after he left from a meeting at the British Prime Minister's suite, where the senior president Mr. Saito, I heard, was also present.

I estimate that by 7:45PM, which is when the clock hit full stop for the unfortunate Japanese leader, Mr. Judeaux and I had gone up and down the elevator four times with intervals of three minutes, at most, between these uses. I am not specifying these numbers as a proof of my engineer mind, Mr. Fakhouri. I assume, by now, you have calculated, too, the time Mr. Judeaux had spent away from the British Prime Minister and Mr. Saito, who were meeting in the far left end of the *West* Hallway, which is where, if things were up to me, I would place the suspicious radius. *Zwölf.* Twelve minutes, Mr. Fakhouri.

Why is the timing important? I am providing my Canadian colleague with an alibi, which lasted twelve minutes - long enough for that syringe to get inside Mr. Judeaux's blazer pocket. *Am I thinking of someone?* Mr. Fakhouri, I am not in a position to point fingers at other leaders. All I know is that on his way to the East Hallway from its West wing, where, I repeat, he last encountered

Mr. Saito, the Canadian Prime Minister had to pass by the Bridge of Nations, that thin corridor that houses the French and the Swedish suite.

But you thought I don't play the blame game? I am involved in no such game, Mr. Fakhouri; let me finish my flow of thoughts. My reference to the corridor bridging the West and the East hallways is a logical inference when we are trying to understand Mr. Judeaux's activities that night. Plus, I am blaming neither my French or Swedish counterparts, because they were not the only world leaders present at the Bridge of Nations at the minutes leading up to 7:33PM. Though I was paying little attention to the voices coming from the center of that corridor, I did see, from the corner of my eye, the American President's large frame, and most certainly could hear the loud voices of both the Brazilian and the South African presidents. You there have at least three suspects that might have snuck in the syringe in Mr.

Judeaux's blazer pocket as he made his way around them to the East Hallway, where he helped me out.

What's this business with trash bags? Das ist eine gute Frage. Good question, Mr. Fakhouri, to which I hope *you*, not me, holds the answer. I am not exactly sure when I was appointed as the concierge of the Corridor of Nations. This sense of duty, I believe, must have dawned on me the moment I arrived to the *Hauptstadt des Libanon*, Beirut. As you know, I had arrived much earlier than most world leaders, sometime before sunset. On my way to *Sternenplatz*, or Nejmeh Square, as you call it, I made sure to ask the convoy to pass by the sandy coastline I had spotted from the plane's window as it was making its descent to *der Flughafen* Rafic Hariri.

My reasoning behind this extra stop lies in the news reports I had received prior to my trip about the rising levels of pollution that your seawaters suffer. *Let's see things for ourselves*, I said to myself. By now, according to the embarrassed expression I see on your face, Mr. Fakhouri, I assume you have an idea of what my brief exploration of your city's only sandy shore has brought to my attention.

This. Don't pull the piece of paper too aggressively, Mr. Fakhouri, because what you hold in your hands is a historical landmark that I will donate to the *Deutsches Museum*, whenever it opens an exhibition for climate change deniers like the American President. This Caramello chocolate bar packaging contains an interesting expiry date, which, if elapsed, would have motivated its possessor to toss it there by the sand. As you're now reading on the back of the packaging, this chocolate did not expire a few weeks or months ago. *Nein.* In 1992.

Donnerwetter! This chocolate bar packaging, which I found at a considerable distance from the water, *so you can't blame your neighbor Cyprus*, was tossed there more than a quarter of a century ago. To put things into perspective to you, Mr. Fakhouri, what you hold in your hand and the Berlin Wall fell around the same time. Upon reading this surreal date, with my feet surrounded by more garbage waste scattered around the sand, I wondered whether I had to hold the government responsible, for neglecting this area for such a long time, or *Mutter Natur* herself for not blowing hard enough to get this packaging flying around some desert in Australia by this point.

Why am I telling you this story, Mr. Fakhouri? My realization of the ecological disaster in Lebanon is central to my appointment as concierge of the Corridor of Nations. From around 7:33PM till 7:45PM, Prime Minister Judeaux and I were transporting the recyclable materials from the unsorted garbage bags of the East Hallway to *Sternenplatz*, by this compound's entrance, where the sole recyclables-only bin is located. This has been my dual preoccupation in this UN meeting, along with figuring out how to, and I say this only because of *your* government's xenophobia, Mr. Fakhouri, dispose of your country's *other* tier of unsorted, unneeded recyclable materials - *your Syrian refugees!*

All this effort because none of your event coordinators were eco-conscious enough to have more than one recyclables-only bin in the radius of a whole kilometer. *Who should I hold accountable for this mismanagement?* Hearing your inability to pull the pieces of this crime together, Mr. Fakhouri, I would suggest a far easier murderer to identify - *yourself*. By the end of this three-day meeting, you will have killed far more trees than Lebanon can support. At this rate, I expect you soon to sign a motion from parliament, calling not for the cessation of tree cutting, since there will be none, but for the cutting out of the only Cedar left in Lebanon - that green drawing on its official flag!

More importantly who I do think the real murderer is? Though I disagree with your way of prioritizing things, Mr. Fakhouri, I might offer you a valuable insight that could help you advance with your investigation. In my brief experience as concierge of the Corridor of Nations, I have come to discover the buried truths about our leaders inside their respective rubbish. In some way, the expression becomes: *Give me your trash bag and I'll tell you who you are.*

For example, yesterday morning, I heard the American President Ronald Chump entering the Canadian Suite under the pretext of needing some moisturizer from the handsome young man. This came to me as a surprise since, the same morning, I had found in the garbage bin by the elevator a half-used jar of moisturizing cream. You don't have to ask me what makes me sure that this belonged to Mr. Chump since it was an American product and had *America First* written in large, much larger in fact than the safety instructions.

But catching the American President's lie strikes to me as trivial. He probably needed an excuse to talk to Mr. Judeaux about the funding of his wall with Mexico. There is a more seemingly significant lie I have also come to expose thanks to my persistence in getting my hands dirty. I mean this *literally*, Mr. Fakhouri, not metaphorically, so enough with the suspicious look. Anyway, this lie concerns the Saudi king, who, along with his Turkish and Iranian counterparts, have made it known to all of us that they are fasting for Ramadan regardless of their duty to be present at this UN meeting.

I can personally confirm to you that the Turkish and Iranian Presidents have been obedient Muslims yesterday. Indeed, your responsible event coordinators made sure to allocate every world leader, *including the Muslims, despite their fasting,* new rounds of *plastic* cups marked with their respective country flags, *every three hours* throughout the day. Ecological genocide right there. Anyway, as expected, I found cups with Turkish and Iranian flags only after sunset, the time they are permitted to start eating and drinking again. But, to my shock yesterday afternoon, I did find a few plastic cups engraved with the Saudi flag. I am positive, Mr. Fakhouri, that the Saudi King must have thrown these cups long before sunset. *Was he breaking his fast?* Very likely. For a loud preacher of Muslim values, I find this to be extremely odd. He could have made it known to us that he wasn't going to fast this Ramadan, exceptionally for the sake of your poor refugees. Unless he planned to break his fast with murder.

THE TRUTH ACCORDING

TO SAUDI ARABIA KING BAKR AL OUD

How did three of my suite's cups end up in the Corridor of Nations' garbage bin?

Your question shocks me, Mr. Fakhouri. *Wajaa, wajaa.* First, I am offended as the head of the Kingdom of Saudi Arabia, to which your tiny country should hold utmost gratitude for *Taif,* the accord signed in the Saudi city to end the fifteen-year Lebanese civil war. Second, I am offended as a fellow Arab, to whom the betrayal of the unity among our nations is a great sin. Who have you been hanging out with in this UN meeting... America, who destroyed Iraq? France and Britain, who colonized the Middle East? Or that trash-sniffing Germany, whose country swore to exterminate Arabs after they were done with the Jews? You will regret asking me about my own trash, Mr. Fakhouri. Once I cease all oil deals with Lebanon, you will remain with nothing to trade with but trash. According to your favorite German Chancellor, there has been a long tradition to that on your littered *Ramleh* coast.

We are both Arabs, Muslims, and Sunnis. Yet your eyes, as I have noticed since the beginning of this three-day meeting, have been drawn to the West. Yesterday, for example, we took the famous world leaders' group picture in the beautiful Nejmeh Square. When we were only just preparing ourselves for the cameraman's shot, a process delayed by the gay Canadian Prime Minister, I heard you mumble the most treasonous words to the French President.

Instead of calling the location we were in with its true name, *Sahat Al-Nejmeh*, you kept repeating how you loved *Place de L'Etoile*. Then you told him about your favorite Beirut coffee shop on *Rue Verdun*. And your favorite road to drive on *Avenue General De Gaulle*. Where do you think you are, Paris? This is treacherous to Arabs, Mr. Fakhouri, and your designation as Prime Minister of an Arab nation is destructive to our collective heritage.

The cherry on the top was hearing you speak with other leaders in English; you kept inserting, as though by instinct, a few French words into your sentences. This made me consider withdrawing all Saudi stakes in Lebanon and leave you run off with the wolves on your own. *And by wolves I mean Hezbollah.*

Am I blowing things out of proportions? At all, Mr. Fakhouri. Another moment that drove me crazy was the time we were discussing the integration of Syrian women in host countries. Besides hearing the endless and meaningless statistics of the Swedish Prime Minister, who is better off in Hollywood with her good looks than in a

UN meeting with her inaccuracies, I tried to brush off constant references from the American President about Saudi Arabia's recent lifting of the driving ban on women. *Sakheef.* He volunteered hosting all of Lebanon's Syrian men if Saudi Arabia agreed to host all the Syrian women and a trillion-dollar deal with Ford Motor Company.

What most infuriated me during this session, though, was your own intervention, Mr. Fakhouri. Ms. Springborg had finished sharing with us her report, Mr. Chump had cracked his routine joke, and then the German Chancellor, in her nosiness for trash and details alike, asked you whether Syrian women had well integrated Lebanese society. Instead of dodging her stupid question, you smiled politely, thanked her for her cue and went on blabbering for a whole half-hour about Lebanon's advancement of women's rights, Lebanese and Syrian with no distinction, including motions that would pave way for civil marriage.

La hawlah wala kowa ela billah. Soon Lebanon will be the hub of the Muslim world for all kinds of illegitimate marriages. Why are you doing this, Mr. Fakhouri, to get your Muslim blood mixed with that devout Christian *Nossa Senhora* of Brazil or to marry the manicured Prime Minister of Canada? *Civil* marriage!

I know the reason. Your policies and your behavior at this UN meeting are reflective of Lebanon's identity crisis. If Lebanon is full of people who love speaking French, marrying whomever they want, and drinking alcohol in nightclubs, *and I still cannot believe that you're serving wine to your guests in this Holy Month of Ramadan*, then why can't Lebanon become a progressive, modern and cool nation such as those in the West?

The more you open up to the habits of such countries, the less you are able to keep Lebanon's historical Muslim identity. There is no way around it. In essence, you are letting the Christians, who are no longer the majority of your population, win. Is this why your government never releases demographic reports, to make those Christians feel more entitled than they should be?

Is this why, and this is what most outrages me, you are giving up on those Syrian refugees, who fled a flood akin to Noah's, in order to re-populate the cradle of civilization with its true and most obedient believers - *Sunnis!* You received a million and a half Syrian Sunnis on a silver platter, Mr. Fakhouri. Enough to bury Christianity among the endless minorities your land possesses. All of this - and yet you are proposing to send them to nations where they will be subject to islamophobia and discrimination!

But am I not also betraying my own Islamic duty by breaking my fast? You are still hooked on this idea of trash and plastic cups, Mr. Fakhouri. *Wajaa, wajaa.* Unlike you, I have been observing one of the five pillars of our faith consistently. I did not break my fast with water from those plastic cups. There are endless reasons that could have transported them from my suite to the hallway's trash bin.

First, it could have easily been the cleaning staff. Only yesterday I heard the American President complaining to everyone about how one of the cleaning workers had thrown out his moisturizer box, though it was half full. Second, it could have easily been that German Chancellor, whose obsession with plastic cups might have driven her to gradually retrieve them from our suites, starting with mine, in order to bring them back with her to Germany and turn them into a piece of art to be displayed at the Deutsches Museum.

But the most compelling threat, I believe, is Iran. Listen to me very carefully, Mr. Fakhouri. There may be a reason that you found my cups in the trash bin outside, and the chance that this event is linked to old man Mr. Saito's death is high. You announced earlier that the cause of my Japanese counterpart's death was an allergic reaction to peanuts, after eating a chocolate bar. You also specified that his death occurred at 7:45PM sharp.

If you were a devout Muslim as myself, you would have guessed that this specific time is not random - it is when the sun set yesterday, when true Muslims could finally break their fast. This is the reason why I, along with Turkish President Mr. Andoghram, were not, unlike other leaders, parading somewhere in the Corridor of Nations at 7:45PM. I was in my suite, praying before I could have my first meal of the day.

Now tell me, Mr. Fakhouri, who would be laughing at this unfolding of events, at such a holy time of the day? *No, not the Westerners.* I believe I may have complained too much about them. The great danger is not in the West, but in the East - Iran. *Isn't 7:45PM also a holy time for Iran too?* You forget a little detail, Mr. Prime Minister. Shiites break their fast fifteen minutes *before*

Sunnis, as a way to distinguish themselves from us. For a long time, they used to break their fast always after us Sunnis, but they changed this habit a few years ago as a way to get Allah's attention first.

Don't you see what this murder is all about, Mr. Fakhouri? I am positive that President Ourani orchestrated this murder to implicate both Mr. Andoghram and myself. Among the three Muslims, he would be the only one who had a solid alibi - since Shiites, unlike Sunnis, break their fast at 7:30PM!

He must have planned a whole series of photoshopped images and festivities of himself somewhere in a distant Hezbollah stronghold having his first *eftar* meal of the day from 7:30PM till 8:30PM, leaving out the possibility that he was executing a murder in the political compound at that time. That is why he planned the murder at 7:45PM. So that the Turkish President and myself would have only just started to head for our first meal of the day - as though we went to break our fast with blood!

But fasting itself could be a strong alibi? It certainly would, Mr. Fakhouri, since he who fasts will be extremely too exhausted by the end of the day to commit any crime. Except, of course, for the suspicious Saudi king, who, apparently, secretly broke his fast with three cups of water. There's my alibi vanished, Mr. Fakhouri. Carefully stolen by the Iranian President. Recycled by the German Chancellor.

THE TRUTH ACCORDING

TO IRAN PRESIDENT AMIR OURANI

Did I tamper with the plastic cups of the Saudi king?

Allah has an explanation for everything, Mr. Fakhouri. Please hear him out before jumping into conclusions about the murder of the Japanese President. I am the person who threw out Mr. Al Oud's plastic cups in the Corridor of Nations' trash bin. Avoid the misunderstanding, please. Though these three cups were indeed in my disposition, I had found them, initially, in my own suite, scattered on my desk as though they decorated a fortune teller's table. There was no note next to the Saudi-patterned cups, and I almost turned around to call out security and alert everyone that the Saudi king was breaking into delegates' suites and distributing his propagandist cups.

That said, once I moved closer to the desk, I realized, to my fury, that the cups were not only arrogantly displaying to me the Saudi Arabian flag, but also contained water to tempt me away from my holy fasting of Ramadan. *Shākh darāvordam!* This, I immediately concluded on the spot, represented an act of war by the Saudi regime, likely coordinated with his Western allies, and about which the Iranian state shall not be silent. I gestured my hands in a frenzy in order to toss the water down the pots of plants. I felt I had to act quick before the moist air of the evaporated water could break my fast.

But my hand stopped cold upon sniffing the intense smell coming from the cups. My eyes went wide, as though I was seeing a genie rising from the cups. What had risen, though, was the poignant smell, not of water, but *alcohol.* At that point, I froze and felt that the whole world, in a new episode of the global conspiracy against our uranium enrichment plants, was once again provoking the Islamic Republic of Iran - this time with their own nuclear weapons, that God-forsaking, devil-rising alcohol!

But the Saudi king also hates alcohol? Though I am sure that Mr. Al Oud would break his fast for low-blow, literal shots of drunken revenge against Iran, because we now rule the Middle East, I agree with you in that the Saudi king may not be the only potential suspect in this Affair of the Plastic Cups. The fact that you are also investigating the murder of the Japanese President makes me wonder whether this clandestine planting of cups inside my suite may be a ruse to get my hands tied to an even more loathsome crime - *murder*! The suspects are countless, since my country has been ostracized in this meeting because of our unwanted military presence in Syria.

Am I then blaming the West? Not necessarily, Mr. Fakhouri. It is very possible that some of Iran's best allies are behind this plot. Let me recall to you a specific moment yesterday, when the world leaders gathered for a group picture in Nejmeh Square. In order to avoid getting Iran once again accused of instilling divisions between the Lebanese, I will not dwell upon the suspicious expression the Saudi king was giving you, Mr. Fakhouri, when you were standing side-by-side with and mumbling something to the French President.

The relevant incident takes place when we were only just beginning to line up for the pause. The Russian President, assumingly taking your advice, gestured me to stand between the Swedish Prime Minister and the Canadian Prime Minister. I did so without hesitation, only to find the incoming American President gazing and walking toward us, as though the contrast between my white beard and traditional Islamic outfit and the two other young and stylish heads of states amused him. Approaching us, he pointed his index, interjecting comments as his hand moved first from Mr. Judeaux, then to myself, then to Ms. Springborg: "The Flirty Kid Down the Block"... "The Muslim Father"... "The Soon-To-Be-Veiled Daughter."

Though the women in the group seemed to have purposely ignored Mr. Chump's joke, the men in the group, and perhaps also that Australian woman, erupted into laughter. *Khar too kharé!* My face turned red and once I turned to you, you informed me that my designated place was actually between the Brazilian President and the German Chancellor, who, judging from their intense expressions, needed anyway someone to mediate between them. It was only when I had come back to my true place that I realized I was tricked. I glanced at the

Russian President and I saw him grinning at me. Check out the cameraman's pictures - you might catch it.

Am I saying that the Russian President was behind the Affair of the Plastic Cups? This is possible, especially if the alcohol in the cups was tested in your labs and found to be the poison of vodka. *But you thought I got along with the Russian President?* This, Mr. Fakhouri, is the reason why things are very complicated. Indeed, a person looking into the Syrian War would naturally conclude that Russia and Iran are the best of friends. But this emergency UN meeting has been revelatory for me. Besides Mr. Yutin's jokes and games with me, our session on the political dimensions of the Syrian refugee crisis has proved to me that our respective states do not share the same vision about the Middle East.

I was seated between the Brazilian President and the late Mr. Saito - *Allah rest his soul* - and you must remember my speech about Israel and its harassing of

Lebanon regarding its newly-discovered maritime resources. I brought this up specifically to show that Lebanon had imminent resources that could help with supporting its Syrian population, and that the problem of refugees could be solved only until Israel's harassment has been addressed, condemned and punished. My speech followed interventions from the American President, who defended Israel and brought up Hezbollah, and, to my surprise, from the Russian President, who completely glossed over the problem I raised about Israel and echoed Mr. Chump's call for Lebanon's political independence.

This moment was poignant, Mr. Fakhouri, because it amplified Iran's fears that our loyalty in Russia is misplaced and could be even abused. How else do you explain the incident at the group photo, or the Affair of the Plastic Cups? This is Russia psychologically and politically blackmailing the Islamic Republic of Iran. Cups of alcohol and Saudi flags in the Iranian Suite? *Na, na.* This is an act of provocation, which, for Mr. Yutin, will be hesitantly addressed by Iran. Shouldn't we be forever grateful to them for helping us out in Syria? If they withdraw their support, Iran would once again become isolated by the whole world and the fiasco of the nuclear programme would repeat itself.

Do I then think that the Russian President, cognizant of Iran's need for Russian backing, is framing me with Mr. Saito's murder? Dozāreet oftād! The complicated Russian-Iranian relation is not the sole evidence to this, Mr. Fakhouri. Another incident during the group photo, which I haven't yet shared with you, is a sentence I overheard the Russian President saying to the old Mr. Saito, as both spoke in Russian given the Japanese leader's fluency in the language. I was speaking with the French President when we suddenly turned around upon hearing the loud voice of the Japanese President, as though he was being defensive over something the Russian had said.

The French President, and myself, then found the two heads of states standing awkwardly opposite each other. A few seconds of silence had elapsed when Mr. Yutin chuckled, breaking the awkwardness, and then pulled the Japanese President close to his chest. I am sure the French President also saw the stern face of the Russian as he whispered a few words to Mr. Saito. I was able to catch them: *Горбатого могила исправит.*

It was only until I later consulted the Russian-speaking Swedish Prime Minister about these words that I understood what Mr. Yutin had told his Japanese counterpart. I had brushed off their meanings then, because they made no sense, but now in light of the murder, they have found new resonance in my head: *Only the grave will fix this hump.*

I'm assuming the hump he refers to is the stalemate we had reached prior to the group photo, where a 7 vs. 7 vote on equally splitting the refugees between us required Mr. Saito's decisive call. *Only the grave will fix this hump.* Now that we are more preoccupied with a funeral than a political accord, the Russian President's plan has succeeded. *Befarmâid.* The hump has been fixed. The grave is ready.

THE TRUTH ACCORDING

TO RUSSIA PRESIDENT VENIAMIN YUTIN

Only the grave will fix this hump?

Hilarious. Your accusatory tone makes me reconsider the relevance of the historical relationship between our countries, Mr. Fakhouri. The Russian Federation has protected your Orthodox Christians since the 1850s and we have welcomed many Lebanese who came to Russia, Christian and Muslims, especially during the many civil conflicts between your fragmented religious groups in this cursed land. No wonder the Phoenicians were the first to build ships and travel the Mediterranean - they must have predicted the impending chaos coming to the Levant.

Anyway, not only are your accusations, Mr. Prime Minister, burning the common history between our countries, but they also undermine the common ideology that bridges us - this awareness of the threat against the West.

I am aware that you, personally, Mr. Fakhouri, are not a fan of the East, whether it is your social reforms to distich Lebanon from its Muslim neighbors, your affinity for whatever is modern, or even your stances on political issues such as the war in Syria. You are probably cursing me in your head at this very instance because I am the person who has ordered troops to get involved in Syria to fight the Syrian rebels and to legitimize once again the leadership of Mr. Assad. That name, alone, must be a curse word for you, Mr. Fakhouri, with its resonance of the Syrian regime's own occupation of Lebanon after the country got out of its civil war in 1989.

My relationship with Mr. Assad doesn't have to affect our own relationship? Of course it does, Mr. Fakhouri. *Само собой разумеется.* There is no beating around the bush with me. You can say it. You, Mr. Fakhouri, an Arab Sunni, must despise Russia's meddling in the Sunni state of Syria, our quenching of whatever flame your fellow Sunnis felt over their non-Sunni leader. You hate Hezbollah, Russia loves Iran, Iran loves Hezbollah - the result, you hate Russia.

I will not be embarrassed if you are genuine with your hate, Mr. Fakhouri, because I know that my vision of the Middle East, at the very least, is shared by its Shiites - that branch of Islam, which, oppressed since its treasonous inception, very much enjoys my country's presence in Syria and our support of Mr. Assad and Iran. Thus you may be the representative of the Lebanese, but your hate toward Russia does not represent the general sentiment in your country.

After all, you are aware that I was the first to arrive among the world leaders - the night prior to our meeting. I went on a special tour of the South of Lebanon, the cradle of your Shia population, and I relished in the ubiquitous Russian flags welcoming me, whether they were hung down the balconies of the neighborhood, against traffic or electric poles, and even posted on the back of old, worn down taxi cabs driven probably by men old enough to have also chanted hymns to Stalin. These men are proof of this counter-culture sprouting in your villages, Mr. Fakhouri - the people who are fed up by the West and its imposing of its own norms and visions upon the rest of the world. You know what's ironic, Mr. Fakhouri? That if the Lebanese people had to choose between my account of Mr. Saito's death versus that of their own Prime Minister - they would pick mine.

Then what is my account? First, let me debunk to your excellency this stupid, overheard idea of humps and graves. The Russian expression *Горбатого могила исправит* contains indeed the word fix, hump and grave - but their combination is lost with whoever translated their meanings. I can venture to say that it might have been the Swedish woman who snitched my name - she proudly informed me of her fluency in Russian and I barely understood five words she has told me since the beginning of this meeting.

Anyway, the expression is used when describing a person who is set on their minds and cannot be changed. It is used fairly colloquially and frequently in Russia. If it meant as you thought it did, Russia today would be a large dump of dead bodies. *What about Mr. Saito's loud shriek?* Да нет. That struck me as normal for a Japanese, Mr. Fakhouri.

Who do I think was behind the crime? Now you are asking good questions, Mr. Prime Minister. I can solve your little mystery because I have the keenest of eyes in this group of blind nations. I suspect that your investigation has mostly focused on world leaders who were around the Canadian Prime Minister by the time of the crime, since your only piece of evidence is that emergency syringe found in Mr. Judeaux's blazer pocket.

This is a wrong approach, Mr. Fakhouri. Even though I share with you the idea that the young Canadian is too posh to have committed the crime himself, and was likely framed for it, I believe you must focus on the true weapon of the crime - the peanut butter chocolate bar that Mr. Saito ate by accident, which caused his allergy to explode.

As you know, before stumbling against the Chinese President and I and dying in front of us at the step of his suite, the Japanese President was attending a meeting at the British Prime Minister's suite. Listen to me very carefully, Mr. Fakhouri. I want you to think of my reasoning against Prime Minsiter Maya Therese without making connections with the whole affair of the Russian spy poisoning. I am not casting my doubts upon that witch of a lady because of her accusations against the Russian Federation. In fact, the evidence I hold against her is based on signs of alliance she has expressed to me, not of enmity. Don't ask why the media would rather talk about the latter than the former.

Indeed, you must be aware of the frustrating behavior of Ms. Therese ever since the beginning of this meeting. Everyone has grown sick of hearing her British accent blaring hysterically in the corridors, repeating on and on the same pitiful word: *Brexit, Brexit, Brexit.* In fact, the reason Ms. Therese is here in Beirut is not to negotiate refugees among us nations but to beg for new trade deals.

Yesterday morning, for example, as I was waiting for the elevator in the East Hallway, I saw Ms. Therese catch the Brazilian President Vilma Yosef, by China's suite, in the middle of her attempt to fix her hair in front of the mirror. The British woman, senseless of her loud voice at such an early time, propelled herself onto her Brazilian counterpart and bombarded her with Google facts about Brazil's banana industry and suggested to her a post-Brexit deal to export them more aggressively to the UK. Ms. Yosef's face quickly grew red, giving the impression that the British witch had caught her in the middle of an important mission she had to abort.

She even managed to harass the American President, who, upon leaving his Canadian counterpart's suite, was intercepted and reminded of how Brits and Americans historically stood together, WW1 to Iraq. When she then suggested that their nations stick together economically, hinting at the increases of trade tariffs that Mr. Chump has threatened about recently, the American President could barely seem to pay attention to her rants.

The distracting delight on his face upon leaving the Canadian Prime Minister's suite only vanished when he smiled at Ms. Therese, pointed at the Chinese President's suite, raised his thick eyebrows and whispered: *We got to stick against them, Mrs. Blair.* The British Prime Minister, yet to register Mr. Chump's name mistake, likely caused from the mention of Iraq, found the South African President and seized the opportunity to harass another BRICS member. Беспредел!

How does Brexit have anything to do with last night's crime? Mr. Fakhouri, from the examples I have just informed you about, I hope you now see the despair of Ms. Therese to form new alliances with emerging economies after Brexit. This despair has very much to do with the crime. Indeed, the British Prime Minister's harassment did not stop at intercepting delegates by the East Hallway's elevators. Did you know what brought the Japanese President to Ms. Therese's suite during the last hour of his life?

A post-Brexit deal with Japan? Correct, but a crucial piece of information that you're missing is the desperate measure the British woman had taken to attract us delegates to her suite. The meeting was open to all the delegates, without exception. *How come Japan was the only one who showed up?* You forget that the Canadian Prime Minsiter was also there, Mr. Fakhouri. What is the common trait between these two world leaders? Their politeness.

So am I saying that Ms. Therese killed Mr. Saito? You love cutting people's speech, Mr. Prime Minister. No. I do not believe that Ms. Therese was that desperate to kill the Japanese President on purpose. It was an accident, and I say this because I still haven't mentioned to you the desperate measure that the British delegate used to attract us to her suite that evening. You must be aware of this anecdote, actually, because you were present.

Do you recall that session about integrating Syrian refugees in host countries' neglected agricultural workforce? At some point, the American President brought up the fact that the USA exported 40% of nuts in the world. When the Australian Prime Minister joked about America's obsession with peanuts and peanut butter in particular, after which Mr. Saito rolled his eyes, as well as the French President, Ms. Therese jumped into the conversation and pledged, though we were talking about exporting *your refugees*, a higher import of peanuts from the US.

The British Prime Minister, as though anticipating Mr. Chump's passion for peanut butter, and forgetting Mr. Saito's allergy, which we had been all informed about, spoke up about Britain's growing love for American peanut butter and pulled up from her purse a PeanuTart bar.

Oh you didn't see that part? This is why you've been struggling in this investigation, Mr. Fakhouri. This is exactly what Ms. Therese was carrying with her during the session - a chocolate bar, made in America, to tempt another man made in America to make a post-Brexit deal. Of course, realizing that her abrupt raising of the bar was rude and perhaps even dangerous to the old Mr. Saito, Ms. Therese immediately put it back in her purse.

But why did she have it there in the first place? This is the desperate measure I have been trying to explain to you from the start, Mr. Fakhouri. The American chocolate bar was not the only foreign product Ms. Therese had brought with her to this tea-time party. In that failed meeting where only the Japanese and the Canadian leaders showed up, Ms. Therese had lined up all sorts of treats and goods from delegates' respective countries - as though to prove to them Britain's commitment to foreign exportation. Brazilian soybeans to please Ms. Yosef. South African grapes to please Ms. Maseko. Even a vodka bottle of Stolichnaya to have me over for a shot.

This is the despair that draws people to commit murders, Mr. Fakhouri - in Ms. Therese's case, by accident. She must have had stashes of PeanuTart bars ready for Mr. Chump. Mr. Saito must have gulped some after Ms. Therese force-fed him entire rolls of sushi from his own country.

There you go, Mr. Fakhouri. Isn't a British person's daily crime their afternoon tea-time? *Bloody* hell yeah. And then they accuse Russia of poisoning people.

THE TRUTH ACCORDING

TO UK PM MAYA THERESE

Was is it my PeanuTart that Mr. Saito chocked on?

Shambles, Mr. Fakhouri, absolute shambles. Your administration has handled this investigation as worse as how my predecessor Mr. Tony Blair handled Iraq, and much worse, surely, than how his own predecessors, a long time ago, handled the Middle East in the wake of World War I. Is it this bitter history between our worlds that lies at the root of your accusation?

Is it because, ages ago, we promised Israel a nation among your lands? Or because of our intervention in Iraq and alignment with this imaginary block, the *West,* toward which you Arabs, though exceptionally, find unity

71

among each other through a common enemy? Is it this enmity which now motivates your accusation?

Well, Mr. Fakhouri, I have news that will cripple your investigation even further. Yesterday evening, I was indeed hosting a late tea-time party to which no one but the Canadian and Japanese presidents showed up - everyone else had other commitments, unfortunately. It is also true that I did have, as a matter of courtesy, appetizers ethnic to the different cultures in this UN meeting. That said, I did receive the memo, prior to coming to Beirut, informing all the world leaders of the senior Japanese President's intense allergy to peanuts.

This is why my tea-time, much to your coming disappointment, did not include any of the PeanuTart bars I had brought with me for Mr. Chump, as a testament to Britain's loyalty for American products. In fact, I still have all those bars with me in my suite, completely sealed, inside my closet. I approached the

American President countlessly about them, but for some reason, whenever I brought up Brexit to him, he would, perhaps out of sympathy to us, lose focus from our conversation.

Am I sure there was no other food in my tea-time that contained peanuts? I still see suspicion in your eyes, Mr. Fakhouri. What I will now reveal to you will further trouble your quest for the truth. During the tea-time, after the Canadian Prime Minister had left to attend, what he called, an *urgent meeting* with the German Chancellor, Mr. Saito and I proceeded to talking about the similarities between Japanese and German economies, which brought a smile to my face because I could see in this wonderful president a powerful ally, a perfect substitute to German economic robustness and engineering prowess, which, because of Brexit, Great Britain has lost.

It was this exciting conversation that, alas, was not only tarnished upon Mr. Saito's later death at the step of his own suite, but had started going downhill when the Japanese President had taken out, after glancing at his watch and stroking his belly, a chocolate bar *from his own* blazer pocket. I was standing in front of him, by the table that held all the cultural savories and sweets, and I could tell from distance that what he held in his hand was not an ordinary chocolate brand - but a PeanuTart bar.

I had barely time to scream out when I saw Mr. Saito, unhesitatingly, eat the whole bar in one mouthful and instantly get possessed by some excruciating feeling. He stood up, his wrinkled face twitching, and he waved his hand in a frenzy, screamed out words in Japanese that I could not understand, and rushed out the door.

Do I think Mr. Judeaux switched Mr. Saito's emergency syringe with the chocolate bar? I don't think so, Mr. Fakhouri. Why would the Japanese President be so eager to eat a chocolate bar that he had just found by chance in his jacket pocket? That doesn't make sense at all. Plus, Mr.

Judeaux is too kind to commit the crime. Canadians, in general, are too nice. Look at the way they achieved their independence from the British Empire. Did you ever hear of a Canadian revolution, similar to America's, or India's? It never had to happen because of how nice and polite Canadians are. Instead of revolting, they chose to wait until the British themselves withdrew from Canada!

This is why I don't believe that Mr. Judeaux planted that PeanuTart bar in the Japanese President's blazer pocket. It must have been someone else, and I believe I know who it was. Before I cast my suspicions, however, I have a question for you, Mr. Fakhouri. Would you be interested to talk about a post-Brexit deal over the exportation of Lebanese soap? My administration is willing to boost the Lebanese economy if we see that a long-term partnership over trading goods can be formed.

Can we talk about this later? Fine, Mr. Fakhouri, I will let you prioritize the murder of Mr. Saito over the reshaping of the whole global economic landscape. Perhaps the discovery of Germany's involvement in the plot could make Brexit, for once, sound like a much better idea.

The person I suspect to be involved in this plot must have willingly given Mr. Saito the chocolate bar. I believe so because it wouldn't make sense that this careful Japanese president wouldn't at least take a second to look at the chocolate bar he devoured in one mouthful. The culprit must therefore be one of the closest people to Mr. Saito, someone he trusted enough to eat whatever they had given him.

This trust, however, does not seem to lie in some strong friendship Mr. Saito had with another leader: he is much older than all the rest so he had no buddies in this meeting, and his professionalism kept him from hanging out with us leaders during break sessions. But this distance is not always true. Did you hear in the news recently, Mr. Fakhouri, about how Japanese people are not having sex?

What does this have to do with the investigation? Listen to me till the end, Mr. Fakhouri. Don't look at me this way - we are grownups; we can talk about sex. I mention this article because it was brought up during the session on the demographic implications to host countries receiving their share of Syrian refugees. The Iranian President warned us that we ought to remember that welcoming hundreds of thousands of Syrian refugees meant welcoming hundreds of thousands of *Muslim Sunnis.*

This, he argued, could greatly disrupt the demographics in the long-term, and could therefore re-configure the voting outcomes in the specific districts where these refugees end up conglomerating together. He then warned us that each nation would have, in a hundred years, their own separatist Catalonia to deal with. Though

Mr. Ourani brought this up for his own sake, because he doesn't want more non-Shiites in his country, and whereas Mr. Yutin joined his Iranian best friend's call for his own obsession with his Orthodox lot, it was Mr. Chump's comment that was the most mortifying. He had said, and you surely remember this: *Just don't let them have sex.*

Uproar exploded in the room. The Swedish Prime Minister grunted loudly and waved her hands in confusion, and the German Chancellor stood up brusquely, kneeled toward where Mr. Chump was sitting, slammed both her arms against the table, and screamed out something in German, which I believed was the word they use for *eugenics*. The French President stood up at that point, hoping to mediate between the two leaders by telling Ms. Angels that eugenics was not what Mr. Chump had meant. Before the American president could shake his head, to say, I believe, that he was *indeed* referring to forced sterilization, the South African President had already stood up from across the room and reminded everyone that of course Mr. Chump was referring to eugenics because his predecessors had implemented them against African Americans.

You obviously remember your own intervention at that point, Mr. Fakhouri, when you called time out and asked everyone to take a fifteen-minute break. You then proposed to accompany the German Chancellor to the restrooms, for her face was fuming red, but she rejected your help under the pretext, and I still don't know what she meant about this, that she had to use this fifteen-minute break to save the planet.

You therefore attended the American President, who, at that point, was blabbering to the whole room that his idea was inspired from an article he had read online about how Japanese people, because of how strict and harmonious their culture was, weren't having sex.

Regardless of whether this is true or not, Mr. Fakhouri, this news, I believe, inspired one of the leaders present to aspire to become the closest person to Mr. Saito - who is old and widowed, I must remind you.

Am I turning this affair into a British domestic drama? Do not discredit the importance of this development, Mr. Fakhouri. All I am saying is that the Japanese President could easily have been fooled, because of his sex*lessness*, by any woman in this meeting. A seductress of this kind, with her ability to get close to Mr. Saito and be a little touchy, could have easily slipped that chocolate bar in his pocket. Maybe this woman was working in a team and was the agent responsible to administer the poison; trick the Japanese president into taking it by choice, rather than force, in order to avoid suspicion. How else would you explain how Mr. Saito unconditionally devoured that PeanuTart? Trust me on this, Mr. Fakhouri. He was under a woman's spell.

Do I then think it's the Swedish Prime Minsiter? Oh that's rubbish, Mr. Fakhouri! I understand that Ms. Springborg's beautiful youthfulness could have tempted Mr. Saito, but I doubt that this moral and respectful young woman has anything to do with this murder. In order to uncover the culprit's identity, I suggest we look at some footage you have of our meetings. Maybe we can spot who has been the closest female leader to Mr. Saito. Maybe we can catch her being touchy with him and slipping something in his pocket. *Eureka!* Mr. Fakhouri, do you possess the pictures we took as a group in Nejmeh Square?

You have them with you? Brilliant. Let us check these pictures. I see there's plenty of them - that's right, we had to take the picture several times because Mr. Judeaux, instead of shooing a passing pigeon, replicated exactly what his ancestors did to my own - wait until it left the frame.

This makes things interesting because we have plenty of seconds separating each picture. Look at this, the Saudi king looks furious as he seems to be staring either at you or the French President. The Iranian doesn't look too happy either. He seems to be turning his head to Mr. Yutin, the one and only friend who bothered conversing with him during the breaks. Here is also the German Chancellor bending down and picking up something she must have dropped. And here is - oh wait, look at this!

What is the South African President doing there? Let me first check the chronology of these pictures. This came first. This one is definitely somewhere in the middle. This came later because the bird was finally outside the frame. OK. I see what is going on here. *Bloody hell.* Do you see this, Mr. Fakhouri? This is as clear as day light. The South African President, Ms. Maseko, has her hand in Mr. Saito's jacket pocket. That can't be someone else's hand because she is the one black person in the group. We solved it, Mr. Fakhouri. This distraction is over. Now how much Lebanese soap would you like to export to the UK?

THE TRUTH ACCORDING

TO SOUTH AFRICA PRESIDENT LEYMAH

MASEKO

How do I explain this picture?

I see what is going on, Mr. Fakhouri. *Haikona*, this is a set-up. A conspiracy against South Africa. Your suspicion shocks me, especially after the efforts of my government to stand against any economic cooperation with your Zionist neighbors. Our nations are friends - or used to be, it seems - because we both had to face and liberate ourselves from the oppressive hands of tyrannical regimes.

If I mention this accusation to the heads of states from the Maghreb and North Africa, who are part of our

African Union and your Arab League, they would be very appalled. In fact, if this accusation compelled them to choose whether to stay in one regional organizational body over the other, I am fairly confident that they would choose to preserve their African allegiance rather than keep their treacherous Arab identity.

Because us African people know what matters to us and how to achieve them. Your failure to investigate the murder of Mr. Saito is a microcosm of the Arab League's own failure, which would rather *observe* conflicts in Syria and Iraq and Yemen and Libya, rather than intervene in them. I do not understand you Arabs, Mr. Fakhouri.

There is an extreme amount of pride associated with this word, *Arab*, almost akin to *African*, yet there is little action done across your nations to achieve something worth being proud of. Whereas Arabs would rather rest on their laurels, and I mean oil, until they exhaust them, look at how us Africans are forging our destinies with our own hands. The difference becomes clear between you and me: an Arab takes pride in what they have, until they don't, an African takes pride in what they don't have, until they do.

Let me explain to you the context of this photo, so I could cast you down a steeper and darker path in your investigation. Mr. Saito and I were indeed whispering words to each other, as you can tell from the way I am jerking my head toward him with my eyes turned to the floor. The secrecy you sense in this picture, however, has nothing to do with the kind of intimacy with which I suspect you are charging me.

In fact, if you would like to find a culprit who has been touchy with Mr. Saito, you are better off asking that witch of a woman, the British Prime Minister, who, since the beginning of this meeting, has been intercepting us by the elevator, one by one, patting us on our backs and on our arms and on our hips when we pretended not to have heard her calls, and asking us on and on about re-negotiating post-Brexit deals. *Domkop.*

This happened to me yesterday, when I was trying to reach for the elevator in the East Hallway. I had heard Ms. Therese's hysterical voice and I was keen on jumping straight into the elevator car without glancing once by the Chinese, Canadian and American suites. What made me turn, unfortunately, was hearing that gross American president, for some reason, address the British Prime Minsiter as *Mrs. Blair.* This took me aback; I glanced for one second to see if he was indeed speaking to someone else, and my eye plunged right into hers - and she started talking.

Anyway, in the picture you hold at the moment, you can see me clearly whispering to Mr. Saito. I assure you, however, that there was nothing intimate to it and that you are better off checking with the womanizer Mr.

Chump should your culprit be someone of this caliber. The reason Mr. Saito and I were standing in this suspicious, clandestine manner is due to the secret nature of our conversation, which we didn't want a specific world leader to overhear.

Across the German Chancellor, the Iranian President, and my darling Ms. Yosef, you will find standing the Chinese President, Mr. Wei. If you re-consult your vast portfolio of pictures, because I know that the Canadian Prime Minister's dandiness compelled us to take many, you would be able to see at least one or two pictures in which I am throwing a quick glance at the Chinese President.

We were therefore, far from talking about sex, discussing an important matter related to China. This brings me back to the session in which we all discussed the political tensions in the Middle East, which, because it naturally crippled the sector of tourism in Lebanon, had a direct effect on the support Syrian refugees could receive.

At some point in the conversation, the two young Swedish and Canadian Prime Ministers proposed a joint motion to revisit the UN's previous failed diplomatic interventions regarding the Middle East, an inaction which they identified to be the root cause of the instability in Lebanon. Each world leader had to respond to the motion, by making concessions about how their states could have better intervened in recent political crises in the Middle East, such as that between Qatar and Saudi Arabia. Instead of speaking about this specific political crisis, however, the stupid American President used his turn to further his agenda to demonizing China. He pointed at both the Japanese and Chinese Presidents and said: *Why talk about solving tensions between Qatar and KSA when we haven't yet solved these guys' problem?*

You must remember the uproar that followed. A succession of interjections splashed between the two Asian leaders, one would scream out *Senkaku* and the other *Diaoyu*, and they would continue to correct each other while gradually raising the pitch of their voices. I really thought at that point that the 80-year old Japanese President was going to chock on his breath, rather than peanuts, and crumble before us. He was infuriated.

At first, of course, I was not sure what they were interjecting, but I then slowly understood that they were both saying the name of the islands between Japan and China whose ownership is contested between the two. Mr. Yutin, at that point, had stood up and pressed his arms against Mr. Wei's shoulders, calming him down, while I called out Mr. Saito's name, rolled my eyes to him and told him not to make a big deal out of an issue that didn't concern us that day.

The hot tempers of both Asian leaders soon calmed down and the American President had stopped poking the issue, for his smile was up to the roof when he delightfully witnessed the exchange between Mr. Saito and Mr. Wei. The way we carried on to talking about Syrian refugees did not bury the issue completely, though. None of the leaders, I believe, had noticed that at some point in our discussion, the Russian President had slipped a note for the Japanese President to read. I may have been the only person to have seen it, since I was seated next to Mr. Saito - who, after my glance, noticed what I had seen.

It was only later on, when Mr. Saito and I were heading outside to gather for the group picture, that he gave me the small note that the Russian President had slipped him. I held it in my hand, but before I could throw a quick glance at it, I had to immediately conceal it when I saw Mr. Yutin heading toward us. My hand had curled into a knuckle, I smiled politely to the Russian President, and let both presidents discuss things on their own. I read the note in private and it was somewhat concise. It said, over Mr. Yutin's signature:

How about we meet at 7:45PM in your suite to discuss refugees and islands with China?

I see an opportunity for compromise.

It was only until Mr. Saito and I reunited for the picture that I was able to slip it back into his pocket. This explains the Affair of the Picture. I am not sure if you can still find the rolled paper in the blazer Mr. Saito wore that day. It has probably been since recycled by Trashella. Anyway, I promise to you, Mr. Fakhouri, that this was the content of the note. My interpretation to it, at that point, was that Russia wanted to broker a compromise between China and Japan over the islands by using this emergency UN meeting as a means. *What would Russia gain from this?* I believe the stakes are obvious to all, Mr. Fakhouri. By the time of the group photo, all us world leaders knew that there was a stalemate over the vote to split the Syrian refugees equally.

Seven leaders, such as myself, had explicitly talked about their opposing of this motion. Russia and China were among us. Another seven nations, like France, Germany and Canada, *those liberals*, had made it known to all of us that they would vote for the motion. Japan, as you noticed, refrained from disclosing which side he was on. Since we had agreed prior to setting up this emergency meeting that a majority vote, regardless of vetoes, would suffice to implement a resolution, Japan's vote was crucially decisive. This is my analysis, which I tried to whisper to my Japanese counterpart in this photo you hold in your hand. Check the next photo in the sequence. You might see me whispering a final thing to

Mr. Saito, with my cheeks twisted with sarcasm. *Good luck with that meeting.* Eina! I guess he didn't have much.

THE TRUTH ACCORDING

TO CHINA PRESIDENT HU WEI

What's this under-the-table deal about the Senkaku Islands?

I am not sure what you mean by this, Mr. Fakhouri. If you are referring to the Diaoyu Islands, part of the People's Republic of China, I am not sure whether your question holds a suspicious tone. I will be honest with you only because I would like to seek justice for my Japanese counterpart, Mr. Fakhouri. The media portrays the relationship between China and Japan as hostile, but my full cooperation with the Lebanese security forces shall prove otherwise.

Yes, there was a deal brewing under the table. *Nà yòu zěnyàng?* Would you expect anything less from a former KGB spy like the Russian President, Mr. Yutin? For as long as I have had to deal with this ambitious man, I often had to be in the awkward position of shooting down some covert discussion he would propose to have with me. And whenever I do so, he keeps bringing up this weird Russian expression of cracking someone's hump and burying them alive.

The truth is that China, though often associated with Russia, is no fool to always go with the flow with it. If he believed in the cause, Mr. Yutin might as well have devised a plan to kill Mr. Saito, or perhaps, as you say, want to solve the island sovereignty dispute in the hopes that the Japanese President votes against the motion to split the refugees equally among us. I wouldn't care less if either or both of these hypotheticals are true because China is involved in neither plots.

Take, for example, Syria. You can see, whenever we hold a UN vote upon the matter, whether China is convinced with Russia's claims or not. Sometimes we did join Mr. Yutin's veto because we felt it compelling - and sometimes, using the best diplomatic tactic, we *abstain*. I thus assure you that if Mr. Yutin had devised any plan of the proportions you describe, China certainly abstained from it.

Plus, the meeting you mention never took place. At 7:43PM, Mr. Yutin and I had left the Russian suite and walked down the West Hallway. We were hearing loud voices coming from the Bridge of Nations but we couldn't care less about them because the supposed argument involved that American clown Mr. Chump.

We were there, by the Japanese President's suite, at 7:44PM - early, or just on time, because we assumed that the Japanese head of state, like his own people, was extremely punctual. The Russian President knocked once

- because we also assumed that Japanese people hated any kind of disturbance of peace. It was some twenty or thirty seconds later that we realized that Mr. Saito had proved to be neither punctual nor harmonious. We turned around us, brusquely, to the sound of a crashing door at the other end of the West Hallway. We then saw Mr. Saito rushing out of the British Suite and spearing forward toward us; he stumbled against us and crumbled at the step of his door.

Isn't it weird that a Japanese person like Mr. Saito would be late to our meeting? I see your point, Mr. Fakhouri, but I believe the explanation for this gap between expectation and reality is quite simple. I remember that the suite Mr. Saito was rushing out of was that of the clingy British Prime Minister Ms. Therese. I bet that this woman blabbered so long about *Brexit, Brexit, Brexit,* that it dazed the Japanese President into forgetting about his meeting with us. It would make sense that the polite head of state would not even have ventured to cut the British woman's speech. How could he when she must have juggled between the vowels of *Toyota, Honda, Mazda and Yamaha?* With that British accent and her desire for exports, she must have been speaking brutally faster that the capacity of all those cars combined.

Mr. Saito would surely have been alive if he had followed my approach with dealing with the British Prime Minister. Yesterday, for example, as I passed the Bridge of Nations to head to the meeting room, I found Ms. Therese harassing the South African President. This proved to me how shameless Ms. Therese's behavior had become, especially seeing her beg for money from the nation her country had plundered the most as a colony. *Suíbiàn.* When she had finished with Ms. Maseko, she turned to me, smiled gleefully, and asked me what was being made in China these days. Though I did not slow down the pace of my walking, I glanced at her for a second, pointed at the Chinese-made hat she was wearing, and told her that these days *everything* was made in China. *Except apartheid*, I shouted out, as I winked at the South African President and walked away.

Do I think Ms. Therese is behind the murder? This might be true if her sole weapon was her tongue. From what I'm seeing, this plot is filled with accurate timings and the one source of delay that has marked this UN meeting has been Ms. Therese's blabbering about Brexit. I also do remember the time she pulled up a PeanuTart bar in the middle of a meeting, when Mr. Saito was present. Her hysterical eyes, I recall, instantly tightened upon noticing how foolish and reckless she was at that moment. After all, we all received a note from your excellency warning us about Mr. Saito's allergy.

That said, I wonder what other preventive measures the Lebanese government could have taken to stop this crime. Ever since my arrival to Beirut, I have noticed the level of disorganization and inefficiency dictating the administration of your nation. For example, I remember when the American President was blabbering to us during one meeting about the light show your Ministry of Electricity produced for him as his plane made its descent.

Because I had taken a morning walk before that session, I knew that what Mr. Chump had witnessed upon landing to Beirut was no deliberate attempt to welcome him with some lights turned on, and others turned off, but rather a display of the Lebanese government's inefficient electricity management. How can you explain the street lampposts I had seen during my morning walk that were turned on in the middle of the day? You switch your lights on in day light and switch them off at night - a country of opposites! *Zhè shì rúcǐ lìng rén jǔsàng.*

I couldn't even correct Mr. Chump when he was boasting about the so-called light show he received because the German Chancellor was carefully listening to him, seeming happy about the lights that were turned off, and I did not dare mentioning to this obsessive ecofriendly woman that I had seen a genocidal lamppost killing her mother nature with its light on in midday!

My point, anyway, is that your government's general mismanagement raises questions about the way you have handled this case. Why, for example, did Mr. Saito only rely on two stacks of emergency syringes, one in his blazer pocket, which he couldn't find, and one in his suite, which he couldn't reach? *You did in fact assign a special guard with extra syringes?* This is news to me. I see. So the Lebanese government did try its best. But what about this guard? Where was he when Mr. Saito needed him most? Was he distracted, or...

What did I just remember? Something crucial to your investigation, Mr. Fakhouri. I remember seeing that guard you speak about. He was indeed standing somewhere around Ms. Therese's suite when Mr. Yutin and I had left the Russian Suite, which is located exactly at the other end of the West Hallway. But this man, whom you have assigned to protect the Japanese President, did not remain at his assigned position the whole time.

As I was pretending to listen to the Russian President's blabbering about some other Russian-speaking province in need of annexation, I vividly remember seeing this guard moving away from his stationed duty and walking toward the Bridge of Nations, that thin corridor from which I could hear loud arguing. I also remember, and I am not mistaken here, the person who, leaving the chaos coming from the Bridge of Nations, stepped into the West Hallway for a second, motioned at this security detail, and coaxed him into following her into the corridor - and away from the British suite, the one place he desperately needed to be at that time.

This decoy, which distracted Mr. Saito's life boat, was none other than that poor Australian Prime Minister, Ms. David. I am a hundred percent sure about this, Mr. Fakhouri. She is in on it. *Dāng rán.* I would bet anything made in China on this. That is, *everything.*

THE TRUTH ACCORDING

TO AUSTRALIA PM JASMINE DAVID

Why did I usher the security guard away from the British Suite?

Your question surprises me, Mr. Fakhouri. It was my understanding that you have already interviewed most of the world leaders before me. I distinctly recall the moment the American President insisted to testify first, blabbering about some suspicious glance he had seen me receive by one of the girls. What about the Brazilian and South African presidents? They must have informed you about the events that brought your very thin, very fragile Bridge of Nations to crack into complete turmoil on the night of the crime. Their snappy characters were undisputedly the catalyzer of the problem - even though I do not believe that their involvement in the late night drama necessarily implicates them in the murder affair.

Someone mentioned an argument on the Bridge of Nations? This person clearly has a lot of drama in their lives to qualify that incident as an argument - it seemed more like a popular uprising to me. Let me set the picture for you, Mr. Fakhouri, and you will begin to understand why at 7:44PM, assuming you are as accurate about time as the German Chancellor, I had to call out the security guard to interfere in the clash of civilizations that your Bridge of Nations proudly hosted on the night of Mr. Saito's death. If I were to assume that you have so far received conflicting accounts from the heads of states at this UN meeting, it would then seem appropriate to say that even the Japanese President's tragic death could not unite these world leaders.

Much earlier than 7:44PM, I was at a meeting hosted at the Swedish Suite. Ms. Carolina Springborg, a wonderfully gorgeous young woman, had invited me earlier during the day and she made sure to also bring along the Brazilian President, Vilma Yosef, and the South African President, Leymah Maseko. Indeed, Mr. Fakhouri, it was a girls-only meeting.

The exclusiveness of the gender is by no means coincidental - all three of these women, as you have noticed from the session we had on Syrian women, are staunch feminists - of the sort we've seen from the second wave, if not feistier. That said, I must single out Ms. Springborg, because her cool Swedish temperament, generally at least, contrasted with the other two hyenas.

The reason she invited us to her suite had initially nothing to do with Syrian women or women's liberation. Ms. Springborg had informed me that she wanted to convince the South African President to vote for the resolution to split the refugees equally among us nations. She and I, as well as the Brazilian President, who seems close to Ms. Maseko, would attempt to have a *civilized conversation*, as Ms. Springborg called it. Since there wouldn't be the constant sexist jokes of Mr. Chump, *which I'll admit were sometimes quite funny*, nor distracting geopolitical tensions in the world, we might finally discuss the fates of these refugees with the level of responsibility that their plight warrants.

Despite the Swedish woman's genuine intentions and her dedication for the predicament of your refugees, this charitable meeting was quick to derail into a hate meet-up against the disgusting *American bufão*, in Ms. Yosef's own words.

Do not ask me how the focus of the conversation shifted so drastically. All I remember was listening passively to Ms. Yosef's scattered complaints about Mr. Chump - and seeing her get upset whenever I would fail to jerk my head mechanically in revolt upon hearing her stories. *Was she expecting me, like her, to get so caught up with the American President?* Her comments, which sneaked up on us whenever Ms. Springborg would try to form logical arguments to the South African President, grew in tone and in aggressiveness the more we seemed to be less preoccupied by them.

The Swedish Prime Minsiter soon grew tired of Ms. Yosef's complaints and sought, in her diplomatic habit, to perhaps address the concerns about Mr. Chump entirely until we could all go back to talking about refugees. It was this act of Scandinavian politeness, unfortunately, that stripped us of any hope for a resolution because it opened up a Pandora's box blaring with samba music that completely possessed the Brazilian President in her endless rant about the *poor unity among women at this meeting* and the *victory of patriarchs like Ronald Chump.*

Somewhere along her monologue, I motioned to Ms. Springborg, who had exhaled of desperation. I glanced at her suite's door and gestured her to join me for a side-bar so we could discuss how to more effectively re-configure and run an urgent conversation that had fallen under the tyranny of Ms. Yosef's unproductive lash of feminism. She nodded, excused herself an endless time to the Brazilian President, who at that point was indulging in her buddy Ms. Maseko's active listening, and Ms. Springborg led me to the door and opened it carefully with her soft hands.

What she opened to, however, in our attempt to run away from endless jabs at Mr. Chump, was not an empty corridor to escape into - but Mr. Chump himself. You must understand, Mr. Fakhouri, that what followed happened within seconds. Ms. Springborg jumped out, completely taken aback from the way the American President appeared so close to us from nowhere. She had also let out a soft scream out of pure shock, not merely because she had opened the door to a flashing imposing figure like Mr. Chump's, but also following the words shouted out by the American President when she had, in the nick-of-time, opened the door to him: *I'd grab her by the pussy.*

Explosion. I could not remember what happened first: Ms. Springborg moving away from Mr. Chump's face, or seeing her being pushed away by the spiraling bull that was Vilma Yosef. Loud screams. Nails raised up on the offensives. A slamming door. The Brazilian President, as though the words she heard from Mr. Chump had been enough to possess her for real this time, pushed the man who stood so close to the safe space against him she was indulging in and moved him with all her force into the center of the Bridge of Nations. The American President, completely speechless and defenseless, could only hold his hands up as though predicting that he was going to receive a physical blow from Ms. Yosef.

Thankfully, the Brazilian warrior limited herself to pushing her biggest nightmare away and shouting hysterically at him. Of course, none of us present, nor Mr. Chump, understood what the woman was shouting out because it was all in Portuguese - but anyone with little experience of Latin American soap operas would have at least understood the sentiment. The one familiar line would be this *Nossa Senhora* lady she kept invoking as she gestured aggressively with her hands at Mr. Chump, who by this point, had uncovered from his numbness and seemed to be enjoying the escalation of events he had caused seemingly unwittingly.

It was the delight on his face, Mr. Fakhouri, that compelled me to rush to the West Hallway, where I had spotted the security guard when I initially left my suite to head to the Swedish Suite. I predicted that Ms. Yosef's composure at restraining herself from hitting the American President would soon loosen and break when she notices that her fierce resistance was meeting some sexual fantasy in the American President's mind. As you described, I stepped into the West Hallway, hurriedly gestured to the security guard, and joined him as we walked straight into the Bridge of Nations to stop the divine retribution impending upon the American President's body after Ms. Yosef's endless saintly callings, from Santa Senhora to *Santa Trashella* - not sure if I am saying the name right of this other mysterious saint she has kept evoking in the past three days.

That said, when I turned to see the latest development between Mr. Chump and Ms. Yosef, though I had been gone only for a few seconds to call the guard, I was shocked to see how things had escalated so quickly. The physical blow I had anticipated against the

American President indeed arrived and with more force than I had expected.

What a slap. You could see Mr. Chump's whole face redden instantly as the hand crashed against his cheek. But to my shock, and this, Mr. Fakhouri, may be relevant in your investigation of Mr. Saito's murder, the person who had exhibited her potential for violence was not the Brazilian President Vilma Yosef.

It was the *civilized* Scandinavian. I swear to you. Didn't you say the other young and polite person at this meeting, the Canadian pretty boy, is also in on it? There you go, Mr. Fakhouri. Your plea for help with your Syrian refugees seems to have perfectly resonated with these two young, passionate, and clearly reckless heads of states. They must have planned this together because of their joint frustration and their failed joint motions at this meeting. Oh millennials. Social justice *warriors*, huh?

THE TRUTH ACCORDING
TO SWEDEN PM CAROLINA SPRINGBORG

Why did I slap the American President?

You had to remind me about this, didn't you? I can still replay the scene in my head, Mr. Fakhouri, and I cannot emphasize to you how ashamed I am. All the self-will I have forged throughout my youth, the composure, the need to stay calm in times of crisis - all evaporated, upon that famed slap! You know, Mr. Fakhouri, I am no believer, as most Swedes I hope, in superstition or phenomena unknown to and unverifiable by science. That said, there is this haunting spirit I have felt on my shoulder ever since my arrival to the city of contrast, Beirut.

I don't know how to explain this to you, Mr. Fakhouri. Somehow, from the moment the driver of the Swedish Embassy passed through that beautiful Cornish with these beautiful yet helpless refugees, and through the endless rival-ridden geopolitical concerns we had to entertain before extending a wishfully-easy hand to this marginalized population - I have felt as though, and the atheist in me hates hearing this, I was venturing into lands that were both holy and *doomed*. A small nation drowned in its boundless history. A people confused as to who they were, and more importantly, who they should be.

I am sorry, Mr. Fakhouri. I am speaking both my mind and my heart to your esteem - I know that this predicament is something you know all too well. The slap you mention, perhaps, was the inevitable culmination of this spiraling trajectory of hope and disappointment I have had to endure during my time in Beirut. I must mention that it has nothing to do with Mr. Saito, if this is what I understand from the suspicion in your question.

I am aware that the uproar in the Bridge of Nations distracted the guard assigned to protect the Japanese President. But I had no involvement in this plot - in fact, nor did this pitiful American President, if you decide to cast suspicion upon him. The falling out between myself and my American counterpart had been overdue - it is a crime in itself that has been boiling ever since the first session at this meeting. You must have spotted the entangling ingredients to this final product. Mr. Chump's nauseating misogyny, my willed composure, and finally, Ms. Yosef's radical feminism, which, I speculate, was the motor that drove me to leap into uncharted territories and, unfortunately, physically abuse the American President. My apologies about that, once again.

Though my innocence, of course, is to be confirmed only by yourself, Mr. Fakhouri, I would like to venture helping you with this investigation. Forgive me if my thoughts are all over the place - I have been trying to figure things out ever since Mr. Saito's death at the step of his suite's door.

Who, among us, would resort to such a desperate act? The thoughts I have entertained have ranged from accusing the desperate British lady, who might have fallen out with her Japanese counterpart over a post-Brexit deal, to accusing the Iranian president who, as though to cast the suspicion on Mr. Yutin, out of the blue asked me yesterday to translate an ominous Russian expression that involved breaking someone's hump. My personal investigation has been futile because I could not place a motive to this killing - it was so senseless that it reminded me of the Islamist extremists we have seen in Europe, who would sacrifice themselves for some heavenly compensation.

This comparison with the Islamist extremists, Mr. Fakhouri, helped me better understand the similarly international yet extremely local crime that your West Hallway witnessed yesterday night. Do you remember the session we had about Syrian women? I was explaining to the table the successful integration of Syrian women into the Swedish economy when the German Chancellor veered the subject toward the integration of Lebanon's own Syrian refugees. Do you remember what you talked about then, Mr. Fakhouri?

Yes, about the advancement of women's rights in Lebanon. While you were detailing to us the remarkable, though unfinished, achievements of your administration, I made sure to keep a hawk's eye upon the three individuals that might have been sensitive to your speech: the heads of states of Iran, Turkey, and Saudi Arabia. My Iranian counterpart, to my surprise, sometimes nodded in agreement with some of the things you mentioned. This was odd given Iran's terrible record with women's rights - but somehow what you mentioned resonated with Mr. Ourani, even though most of the time he would shake his head, perhaps too mechanically, when he turned to the Russian President.

It was the Saudi king's reaction that most frustrated me. You should have seen the glaring stare he was projecting onto you when you were speaking, Mr. Fakhouri. It was as though the basic human rights you were mentioning, *extremely basic*, outraged him. Of course, I am versed enough in Middle Eastern politics to know that Mr. Al Oud's single opinion matters a great deal to the Lebanese women awaiting their rights. How then would you explain the delay of your administration to grant a Lebanese mother's right to pass down her nationality to her children? It must be the pressure you are receiving from religious zealots like the Saudi king - no matter how modernized he has suddenly proclaimed himself to be.

This modernization is a sham, I guarantee you. I have heard him mumbling endlessly to the Turkish President about the usefulness of Syrian refugees to the demography of Lebanese society, a humanitarian aid masking a tribal mentality of *Muslim Sunnis First*. This obsession with demography must also be the reason behind your administration's delay regarding the Lebanese Women Nationality Bill, which would shift things demographically because of the Lebanese women who are married to Muslim Sunni refugees from Palestine, who, foreshadowing the Syrians' fate, are still marginalized in Lebanon since Israel forced them away from their homeland.

This obsession with one's religion is what drives me crazy. It is the source of most of the evils in the

Middle East, I believe, as well as the motor that drives Islamist extremists to commit desperate acts in the name of a religion that cares little about their welfare. Perhaps this is why I have felt doomed ever since arriving to Lebanon - whatever atheism I believe in, it could stand no chance to the endless reminders of some holy fate that bounds the people of these lands. I wish you had sat me away from the Saudi and Turkish leaders - I wouldn't have overheard the endless, depressing chitchat between them.

For example, they would keep referring to the Canadian Prime Minister as *the gay one* and I would cringe my teeth every single time, not merely from their mutual homophobia, but more so from the Saudi king's hypocrisy. We all have been hearing the rumors that he had been breaking his dutiful fast all along with chugs of water cups. Islam becomes this paradox: the bad Muslims are the refugee, the woman, the homosexual - but never, *Allah* forbid, the King.

So am I blaming Mr. Al Oud for the crime? Not quite, Mr. Fakhouri. There is another Islamic clerk in this meeting that I have not yet dwelled upon and whom I have compelling evidence against: The Turkish President. At some point in our conversation, when you mentioned to me that the Chinese and Russian presidents had also witnessed my falling out with Mr. Chump, I remembered an important detail about these two leaders that the South African President had told me about back in my suite before we confronted the sexist American. You can fact-check with both Ms. Yosef and Ms. David on this: she informed us, in a joking manner, about the little note the Russian President passed to the Japanese President. It was about a meeting he set up to mediate between him and the Chinese President - and I vividly remember Ms. Maseko saying that the meeting was at 7:45PM.

As I'm thinking about this now, Mr. Fakhouri, the timing makes me uncomfortable. Isn't it odd that an organized and punctual person like Mr. Saito wouldn't have left much earlier from the British suite to welcome his guests? You said that he rushed outside at exactly 7:45PM - so if we remove the whole allergy situation, he probably either would have left the suite at exactly 7:45PM, which is de facto still rude in Japanese standards, or worse, make it back to his suite a few minutes late. *Don't I think the British woman's blabbering about Brexit could have restricted the polite Japanese?* This was shamelessly my thought too, Mr. Fakhouri. But I have just remembered something very disturbing that shifts the blame.

There is a reason why Mr. Saito was late for his meeting and it had nothing to do with the Japanese President. In fact, Mr. Saito *didn't even know* that he would be late for his meeting at 7:45PM. The pertinent moment I will evoke to you, Mr. Fakhouri, occurred when we were preparing for the group photo at your wonderful Nejmeh Square. If I am not mistaken, before pausing to take the picture, Mr. Saito was conversing with the Russian president - probably about that meeting. He then separated from his Russian counterpart and they both joined the rest of us for the endless pictures we were about to take.

After the picture, I was distracted by the Iranian President, who kept asking me about this weird Russian expression about cracks and humps. But now that I look back, throughout my distracted conversation with Mr. Ourani, my eyes were captivated by a shiny thing that the Turkish President was handing Mr. Saito at that moment. It seemed like a watch. I am not sure if Mr. Saito accepted this supposed gift from his Turkish counterpart. If he did, I wonder if he was wearing it during the night of the crime.

You have his possessions with you? By all means, show them to me. Though all watches look the same these days, I believe there is a specific way to tell if this is the same watch as the one Mr. Andoghram handed to him yesterday. Oh yes. This is it. *How can I tell?* Mr. Fakhouri, I can't believe you have been so accurate with timings in this investigation and yet failed to tell the time on the victim's own wrist. This watch, which the Turkish President gave to the punctual deceased man, does not read the actual time.

It's way behind. Don't look at me this way, Mr. Fakhouri. The intolerant, sexist and homophobic Muslim clerk is busted. Why the hell would he tamper with Mr. Saito's gift-watch? Busted indeed. As you folks love to say... *God*, or for me, karma, is indeed *Great.*

THE TRUTH ACCORDING

TO TURKEY PRESIDENT RAYEF ANDOGRHAM

Did I change the time on the watch I gave Mr. Saito?

Yes, Mr. Fakhouri. I am not ashamed of this fact - if you had interviewed me before all these infidels, I would have gladly confirmed to you this. But of course, once again, Lebanon chose the West over the East - as though it could slip into that small opening of the Mediterranean Sea and escape the chains that bounds it by land to its neighbors. *Her neyse.* You gave in to Mr. Chump's rants about testifying first and dedicated your time hearing from all those nations that screwed over Arabs as yourself ever since they first cast eye on the Middle East's resources. The fall of the Ottoman Empire remains the region's biggest curse. Look at Iraq, Syria, and your own country, Mr. Fakhouri... are you not nostalgic of the peaceful times that the Ottomans blessed upon your lands? Clearly, you do not even see the potential of a strong alliance with Turkey since you have prioritized everyone else but your own Sunni brother.

Well, unlike you, I do not let down my duty to Islam and to real Islam, that is *Sunni Islam*. I did change the clock. If you had been a better Muslim, Mr. Fakhouri, you would not have lost all this time bumping into dead-ends by fixating yourself on meaningless details such as the Affair of Mr. Saito's Clock. It is set fifteen minutes before the current time and the Japanese President rushed out of the British suite at exactly 7:45PM. Doesn't it add up in your head, Mr. Fakhouri? *Infidel.* You are no true Muslim, Mr. Fakhouri. Your love for the West has made you forget your faith. If you cared any less about Islam, you would have guessed that the reason Mr. Saito rushed out at this specific time was because he had eaten at the time Sunnis break their fast. Yes, Mr. Fakhouri. The infidel Buddhist President was fasting.

This horrendous decision was made during breakfast hour yesterday. The American President cracked a joke about whether the Saudi king would be down to go with him to Beirut's notorious nightlife district, Mar Mikhail, and this is when Mr. Al Oud laughed things off and announced that he was fasting for Ramadan and that going would break his fast. I am pretty sure Mr. Chump had received the memo that the Saudi and Turkish Presidents, as well as that traitor Iranian, would carry on their fast despite this emergency meeting - he surely wanted to embarrass the Saudi king, who had a few minutes before Mr. Chump's suggestion talked about being more moderate than his father.

This exchange shifted the side conversations during breakfast. Everyone suddenly was interested in the

Muslims, in how they could *not even drink a drop of water* during the whole day. Mr. Saito was the most fascinated, nodding his head in awe as he spoke with the Iranian President. As he listened, the old Japanese President glanced at his untouched breakfast plate and, as his face flushed in embarrassment, moved it aside and declared proudly to Mr. Ourani that he would fast today in solidarity with him and the one billion Muslims in the world. The Iranian President smiled with delight, wished that everyone would follow the example of tolerance displayed by the veteran Japanese President, and informed him that he could break his fast at 7:30PM sharp. *Bu çok sinir bozucu.*

I had overheard this awful deal between the two presidents and decided that I had to act in order to save the dignity of our faith as well as the dignity of this esteemed Japanese President, who couldn't see the evilness behind his Iranian counterpart. Not only was he ignorant of Iran's devilish plans for the Middle East, but he also didn't know that he would break his fast at the wrong time - at the Shiite time, not the true, Sunni Muslim time.

After our Sunni-only meeting, with you, Mr. Al Oud and myself, where we discussed the Iranian threat in the region, I had made up my mind - I would propose the watch as a gift to Mr. Saito, thanking him for fasting in solidarity with us Muslims, and setting it fifteen minutes before actual time, so that Mr. Saito would break his fast at 7:45PM, not 7:30PM, which was the time he thought he ate that chocolate bar.

This is the full story, Mr. Fakhouri. The Turkish government has nothing to do with the murder - if anything, we spared this poor Japanese man from dying in shame. At least, thanks to my effort, he died as a true Muslim - one who fasted the whole day and ate at the appropriate time. His body may now rest in peace. *But we must find who wanted him dead?* Mr. Fakhouri, I believe I can guide you in your investigation. Allah has not been helping you much because of your infidelity - but Allah is merciful and I, as an obedient believer in his unchanged word, will bow down and help a person as undeserving as yourself.

I believe you have been too preoccupied with timings in this investigation. I do not blame you since the murder had to occur at 7:45PM, a too-specific time in line with sunset hour yesterday. Whoever plotted this, therefore, knew that Mr. Saito was fasting in solidarity with Muslims and that he would probably not double-check whether the chocolate bar planted in his blazer jacket contained peanuts. The fasting is the key, Mr. Fakhouri. Remember, Mr. Saito is 80 years old. I am 50 years old and I get so exhausted by sunset.

The Japanese President must have been so tired that he devoured whatever was in his pocket in one mouthful. These are all logical inferences that a person could make upon the knowledge of Mr. Saito's fasting. I do not remember who had also overheard the conversation between the Iranian and Japanese presidents. That said, there is a specific moment I do remember that could offer you the key to your investigation.

Do you remember the session we had about the potential integration of Syrian refugees into the host countries' agricultural economy? The Australian Prime Minister joked about America's obsession with peanut butter, Mr. Chump boasted about his country's peanut exportations, and that is when that foolish British Prime Minister pulled up one PeanuTart bar to kiss the ass of her American colleague.

After this debacle, ended by the woman's realization of Mr. Saito's allergy, all of us resumed our normal meeting and talked about Syrian refugees - except for two specific heads of states. The American President and the French President, despite our resuming of the session, lingered on chatting, this time in whispers - and I heard the mention of peanuts at some point. They seemed passionate as they spoke. I am not sure exactly what was being said between them, but I do remember how their whispered chit-chat came to an abrupt end.

Their murmurs were loud enough that they stirred the German Chancellor, sitting next to them, who immediately told them off. She was even backed by her nemesis Ms. Yosef, who seemed so anxious to jump at any chance she could get to attack her American counterpart. This is when both presidents finally stopped mumbling to each other and remained silent throughout the session, which lasted some ten more minutes. No one wondered how come neither of them participated as much in the discussion, despite its relevance to both their countries' economies.

I was going to propose discussing the French and American agricultural sectors when I spotted something unusual going on between the two heads of states. I noticed both leaders glancing at each other and smiling at the German Chancellor, who was too preoccupied by her Canadian counterpart's blabbering about some new link between agriculture and sustainability.

At that point, I could not tell what exactly was going on between the French and American Presidents - they were being very discreet. It was only when we broke off for a new break session that I made sure to keep my gaze focused on both of them. I am glad I remained vigilant because that is when I noticed a small piece of paper being raised up and down by Mr. Chump as he laughed with the French President.

This sight made me wonder what Mr. Chump and Mr. Navron had written to each other, what could possibly be so pressing to discuss in a conversation so abruptly cut by the German Chancellor. Of course, I assumed that there was no way for me to obtain this piece of paper because I had seen Mr. Chump leave with it in the distance and I could not follow them because the British Prime Minsiter had intercepted me standing alone and had started blabbering about Brexit and some invitation to a tea-time party she was having.

Why was I so interested in this note? Benimle dalga mı geçiyorsun? Mr. Fakhouri, our Middle East has been shaped by pieces of papers and scribbles of conspiracies secretly passed between countries in the West. Reminder: Sykes-Picot, the secret agreement that divided our nations after WW1. I continued to think about this piece of paper long into the day until a great realization dawned on me.

Where could I find it? Where would this small piece of paper end up? I didn't need too much time to figure out a solution. I was heading back to my suite when I saw from the corner of my eye a short woman carrying trash bags into the corridor. *Eureka, Trashella!* I was convinced about this - the piece of paper must have ended up in the only recyclables-only bin in this compound, outside, by Nejmeh Square, the place Ms. Angels kept flocking to and from to save the planet.

It didn't take me too long to sort through the garbage, which was so impeccably organized as though it was a German-made fridge of a person with OCD. Paper documents were piled up together and plastic cups were folded up against each other. Though finding the plastic cups of King Al Oud threw me off at first, I couldn't care less when I found what I was looking for. Here it is, Mr. Fakhouri.

His excellency still hasn't had his long-awaited PeanuTart bar.

Meet me at Nejmeh Square at 7:00PM.

You will thank America for this.

(and for WW1, of course)

See, Mr. Fakhouri? I know the British Prime Minister also had PeanuTart bars with her. But the sole victims of her harm are everybody's ears. It's these guys who did it, another English-speaking Mr. Sykes and another Frenchman Mr. Picot. History would have repeated itself if it weren't for me. Another secret Western deal would have derailed any hopeful advancement in the Middle East. Do you regret not interviewing me first, Mr. Fakhouri? Sunni Islam is the truth, indeed.

THE TRUTH ACCORDING

TO FRANCE PRESIDENT MANUEL NAVRON

How do I explain this note?

Merde.

There seems to be a misunderstanding, Mr. Fakhouri. This note is not what you think it is - do not associate the usual vague wording of Mr. Chump with this specific case in your hands. I am not sure who provided you with this note, which I remember handing back to the American President. I suspect that Mr. Chump, considering his decision to pull out from the splendid *traité* on the environment we signed in Paris a few years ago, must have thrown it in the normal garbage of the *Couloir de l'Est* and it was picked up by the German

Chancellor. I doubt, however, that Ms. Angels handed this to you, Mr. Fakhouri. It could be the British Prime Minister, Ms. Therese, who would hope to blackmail its age-old rival, *France*, and extort us for a better Brexit deal.

At the same time, I am inclined to suspect Mr. Al Oud, the Saudi king, given the recent feud between him and myself. You, Mr. Fakhouri, were in the middle of this controversial and somewhat politically-awkward stand-off between the French and Saudi governments.

Do you recall this event? It was when your predecessor was stranded in Saudi Arabia and could not return to Lebanon - a political blackmail from the Saudi state, which has been interested in Lebanese political affairs ever since the Islamic Revolution in Iran. *Mon pauvre Liban!* A small nation trapped between the claws of two empires - unable to grow, unable to rise, until the chains that bounds it with its neighbors are cracked and liberated.

But hold on to hope, Mr. Fakhouri. If this note in your hands was indeed handed to you by Mr. Al Oud, still bitter of the way France liberated our historical friend Lebanon, then do not worry - the French government shall not be victim of this Saudi blackmail, nor will it let Lebanon be caught in the middle of the limbo. After all, you must be familiar with international politics, Mr. Fakhouri.

A feud between states is one thing on television, but it is very much different in person, when heads of states deal with each other face-to-face. My relationship with the Saudi King is as flexible as it is with the American President, with whom I disagree on most policy and value levels, but with whom, as this note admittedly attests, I also share a more personal bond.

Let me recall to you the context from which this small piece of paper has risen. Perhaps the person to blame for its writing would be yourself, Mr. Fakhouri.

How could you, in whatever uncalculated pre-arrangements made by your event team, place a disciplined German Chancellor sit next to a loud-mouthed and imprudent American and a careful but curious Frenchman?

If I remember well, we had all been discussing solutions to integrate Syrian workers into host countries' agricultural economies. One joke about America's love for its peanut exports and Mr. Chump couldn't stop talking about peanut butter. *Dégoûtant*! What made matters worse was not the American's love for this strange spread but rather Mr. Chump's insistence on spreading this love to the least likely person on the table - *un Français*! In France, we do not see the culinary appeal of this odd mix - it is a lazy breakfast or a lazy dinner, at most, and if time pressed us, we would much rather spread *Nutella* on our morning *tartines* than to start our day with such a tongue-drying mixture!

It is this gastronomic disagreement between Mr. Chump and myself that catalyzed the story of this note in your hands, Mr. Fakhouri. Our whispers prior to the German Chancellor's definitive hushing involved not a conspiracy over a murder but a debate, banally, over the primacy of either Peanut Butter or Nutella. It is this simple, Mr. Fakhouri, I assure you. Let us read out again the content of your note:

His excellency still hasn't had his long-awaited PeanuTart bar.

Meet me at Nejmeh Square at 7:00PM.

You will thank America for this.

(and for WW1, of course)

I assume things are clearer now, Mr. Prime Minister. When Mr. Chump wrote *"his excellency"* he did not mean at all the Japanese President. I am the head of state which he refers to, the person who hasn't yet had the famous American chocolate bar, PeanuTart. Our meeting together at 7PM, as a result, consisted simply in our desire to leave this political compound and visit the special convenience store your administration has placed by Nejmeh Square in service of the meeting's heads of states and their security and service staff.

We walked together to this small boutique, discussing along the way the tariffs Mr. Chump had threatened to impose on global trade. To tell you the truth, Mr. Fakhouri, it is these tariffs that constitute my motivation to please the American President and to bear listening to his obsessions and rants. Once again, as I mentioned before, state and personal affairs often conflict in our field.

Especially with Mr. Chump. Do you think I could lay out the economic benefits of avoiding a trade war with China to someone who believes that China itself is behind climate change? Nodding to this man-child, thus, was the only way I could take to go along with Mr. Chump and dissuade him from reckless state decisions holding global consequences.

Between politely smiling at some jokes about the Saudi and Iranian leaders, to briefly answering some awkward questions about what I thought of the Swedish Prime Minister, the stroll to the convenience store went somewhat OK. Mr. Chump then brought from the store, recklessly as usual, around ten bars of PeanuTarts, while I only treated him with one Nutella-filled bar because I did not want to be charged, rather than Saito's murder, with the sudden death of an overweight American president from diabetes.

After much harassment to have more than one PeanuTart bar, to prove that I had indeed liked it and would convert from Nutellaism to Peanutism, *and these were his own terms*, Mr. Chump and I walked back to the compound and decided to continue our chat about tariffs in the French Suite. I was at first worried that the American President would decline my invitation to talk about tariffs, but Mr. Chump was somehow very delighted about this idea. He even asked me whether my suite was big enough to fit more delegates. I wasn't sure if this showed his readiness to negotiate global tariffs or simply his weird obsession with room measurements.

Looking back, of course, we all know that this important talk on tariffs never happened. What first delayed this event was Mr. Chump's refusal to enter the French Suite, which I had left, after much coercion from the German Chancellor, without a running air-conditioner in my absence. While I entered first to turn it on, the American President preferred to hang outside my suite, in the always-air-conditioned Bridge of Nations.

Typical from him, he not only delayed his grand entrance to my suite but also decided to continue our conversation from where he was standing. Once again, though, instead of talking tariffs, Mr. Chump went back to talking about the beauty of the Swedish Prime Minister. Since he was standing outside, he must have noticed that Ms. Springborg's suite was opposite of mine and was therefore inspired to obsess about her looks.

I assume you know what happened next. He ended his elegy of the young Prime Minister with a rather unfitting phrase - *I'd grab her by the pussy* - and this happened to be when, as I later understood, Ms. Springborg opened her suite's door and found the creepy figure in front of her. Uproar followed - I remember walking outside upon seeing the Brazilian President, Ms. Vilma Yosef, thrusting forward as a bull toward his matador and pushing the American President away from the Swedish Prime Minister, who could not but screech upon hearing the gross comment addressed to her.

This is my part of the story, Mr. Fakhouri. If I recall right, you have interviewed every head of state except the Canadian Prime Minister, the person that first threw you off to investigating the potential implication of us leaders. I would be surprised if this polite gentleman turned out to be complicit in this appalling murder. But then again, you never know.

Ever since my arrival to Beirut, after all, I have been surprised too many times. Things work in reverse here, don't they, Mr. Fakhouri? A beautiful coastline that treasures chocolate bars that expired in 1992. Street light poles that are turned off at night and turned on in broad day light. A UN meeting of cooperative nations that ends up becoming a clash of civilizations, and a bloody one too. The polite and harmless Canadian is a cold-blooded murderer? Perhaps I should not be surprised at all. Only in Lebanon, as you say.

THE TRUTH ACCORDING

TO CANADA PM LANDON JUDEAUX

First of all, Mr. Fakhouri, I am not gay.

All sorts of rumors have been travelling around your Corridor of Nations ever since our arrival to this inhumane yard sale of Syrian refugees. I am not sure who is responsible for these falsehoods. It must be that intolerant, sexist and in this case, *homophobic* Saudi king - and for revenge's sake, I hail whoever started the rumor against him that he's been breaking his fast with big cups of water. The biggest lies, of course, would be the assumptions against me that I am implicated in the murder of that wonderful Japanese president. All because, according to you, I had in my disposition the emergency syringes that could have saved Mr. Saito's life. This is all, as my American counterpart would say, *fake news.*

Where should I start, Mr. Fakhouri? I wish you had come to me in the first place, although I understand that you would want to get all the facts, and lies, on the table, before consulting me. I cannot guarantee to you that my chronicle of yesterday's events could bejewel you with the name of the real suspect. I will not be like the other world leaders here, who must have pointed fingers at each other, with or without an ulterior motive. I have no interest in incriminating anyone - all I want to do is to tell the truth. The real truth, Mr. Fakhouri, not the Sunni or Shiite one. I've heard enough of those from your Muslim counterparts.

Yesterday morning, the first delegate I met was the American President. My door was open because I was waiting for the German Chancellor to come back with more trash bags. She had informed me of the dire conditions of the compound's almost non-existing recycling system and I agreed to help her throughout the day with her good deeds for the environment.

I am not sure what Mr. Chump wanted from me - I kept looking into the mirror as a means to ignore his usual stupid rants about immigrants or China. Unlike other leaders, whom I shall not name out of respect, I cannot bear listening to this shamelessly politically-incorrect president. A sexist word about the Swedish Prime Minsiter, or an islamophobic rant about the Iranian President, would almost bring me to flames and this would end up having US sanctions crashing not on Iran but on Canada, as a retaliation to my potentially undiplomatic response to the American President.

During the morning sessions, I was present and participating actively, unlike other leaders who, if suspect, would have been too preoccupied with their murder plot to discuss the political climate in the Middle East. The most active delegates in those back-to-back sessions, if I remember well, were the Iranian, Saudi, American and Russian leaders.

I had to keep bringing the conversation back to its original focus, the political climate in the Middle East *as related to Syrian refugees,* but I was overwhelmed by an endless web of hate rivaling in the region: Iran's attack on Israel... America's attack on Iran... Russia's attack on America... Saudi Arabia's attack on Russia. I was happy to finally see Russia and America finding mutual ground, which seems to have upset the Muslim states but that at least put an end to this endless spiral of rivalries that plague the Middle East.

After the morning session, I went on to help my eco-conscious German colleague, by sorting the recyclable material in the Corridor of Nations and transporting them to the only recyclables-only bin in the whole compound, the one outside by Nejmeh Square. Afterward, we were just on time for the afternoon sessions, which, despite some disagreements over how to integrate Syrian refugees in host countries, were successful enough because it seemed that a motion to split the refugees equally among us could pass with enough votes.

Then, you can notice from the pictures in your archives that I was behaving normally during the time we gathered together for that infamous, somewhat hypocritical group photo. You might have seen me halting the cameraman's work because there was a pigeon entering the frame. I did not shoo it right away only because I anticipated the consequences of any drastic movement I made: the bird would have flown up toward where Ms. Springborg was sitting and I certainly did not want Mr. Chump seizing this opportunity to bravely move her aside in order to get his creep's hands on her.

The group picture proceeded normally afterward - except I did hear, according to another rumor, that the Russian President was humping Mr. Saito's back as though he was harassing him.

The second half of the day is perhaps what interests you most. My activities, however, were similar to how the day had started. I resumed my activism with Ms. Angels and this time we had found a few scandalous secrets in people's garbage - once again, for courtesy's sake, I shall not name anybody. Sometimes, the German Chancellor and I opted to strategically split the tasks - she would sort the recyclables, and I would go outside. This is pertinent, Mr. Fakhouri, because this is how I, of all people, would end up in the middle of this murder affair. Please, listen carefully.

When I was by Nejmeh Square to get rid of a batch of recyclables, I noticed chocolate bar packagings thrown in the recyclables-only bin. This struck me because Ms. Angels and I sorted the recyclable material in a very ordered way - paper alone, carton alone, plastic alone. I doubted that the Swedish Prime Minsiter, who also recycled properly, had eaten all those chocolate bars. My doubts were less grounded on the thinness of Ms. Springborg and the multitude of these chocolate bars and rather on the content of one of the chocolate bar packagings.

It still contained half a bite inside. Any person who truly recycled effectively would know that even the smallest organic product inside plastic or paper could tarnish the whole process of recycling. I could not simply remove the chocolate bite because it had started melting and the plastic packaging had been already stained. This is why I picked up this chocolate bar, in its packaging, and held it with me so I could go back to Ms. Angels and have the chocolate bite thrown out and the plastic packaging washed and recycled.

I never made it to Ms. Angels, unfortunately. The British Prime Minister had intercepted me from the elevator, and I was forced to place the chocolate bar and its packaging inside my blazer's pocket and follow her straight to the British Suite, where I promised to attend a meeting on a post-Brexit deal. Though I was expecting everyone to show up to this meeting, for this is the impression Ms. Therese gave me, we were joined only by the Japanese President.

It was rather hot in the room and I wondered whether the desperate British Prime Minister had turned her air-conditioner on low to please the eco-conscious mind of the German Chancellor and myself - a self-interested expression of kindness, of course. Neither Mr. Saito, nor myself, found courage, or time, to interrupt Ms. Therese's blabbering so we opted to remove our blazer jackets to cool down better.

Of course, the spices of the multicultural buffet did not help the atmosphere in the suite - and the steam of the tea brewing had brought Mr. Saito, who looked so exhausted, to finally ask Ms. Therese to raise the flow of air in her suite's ventilating system. Now that you revealed to me that Mr. Saito was fasting in solidarity with Mr. Ourani, his level of exhaustion last night is understandable.

Of course, the poor Japanese could not get anything easy that day. His request for a colder atmosphere had backfired. I assume the British lady's *extreme* willingness to please her guests had pushed her to plunge the suite in extreme cold - and the poor and exhausted Japanese President, at that point, had worn *my* blazer jacket instead of his own, another evidence of how exhausted he had been.

I had enough of Ms. Therese's rants and I really wanted to go back to help Ms. Angels - so, instead of bothering once more the frail Japanese President to remove my jacket, which would additionally strike as uncourteous of me, I opted to wear Mr. Saito's own blazer jacket and leave the British suite.

It goes without saying that I had no idea that the chocolate bar in my jacket contained peanuts - let alone that Ramadan's pre-sunset pain extended to the Japanese *Buddhist* delegate who would devour anything when it was time for him to break his fast. I also hope that you now understand how the emergency syringe ended up in my jacket - it didn't, it was always in Mr. Saito's, which I was forced to wear otherwise I would have been charged with the murder of a Japanese president dead from dehydration.

I assume, Mr. Fakhouri, with things from my end now clear, that your questioning is officially over. Now I shall ask you. ***Who killed the Japanese President?***

THE TRUTH ACCORDING

TO LEBANON PM ADNAN FAKHOURI

Thank you for joining me in Nejmeh Square.

Each one of you has been very helpful and very patient with me as I ventured through this complicated investigation. Your witness accounts, though often in contradiction with each other, have been instrumental to my ability to pull the pieces together. The reason I have taken so long to complete this endeavor lies in the contradictions your interviews have offered me. For example, the evidence the Iranian President provided me with against the Russian leader - *Mr. Yutin, please, focus on me now* - could almost have been a compelling proof of Mr. Yutin's criminal intentions.

But, the translation of the expression he used to Mr. Saito yesterday and which was offered by the not-so-fluent Swedish Prime Minister was not accurate and its true meaning was less harmful than it sounded. Another account that threw me off was Mr. Al Oud's accusation of the Iranian President - the Affair of the Plastic Cups was alarming at first, but it turned out that this plot was not meant to frame the Saudi king but instead to fool Mr. Ourani, a nasty jock played by Mr. Yutin. *Gentlemen, you can discuss this later.*

I mention these contradictions not only to justify the extended time it has taken me to gather you together today, but they are also telling of the general rivalries and tensions in this world summit around a humanitarian crisis that should concern us all. You have said it yourself, Mr. Judeaux, when you described the group photo on these very steps as *hypocritical.* Hypocrisy has indeed shaped the events of this emergency UN meeting. Some of the world leaders who usually considered themselves as friends turned out to be each other's enemies, and some of the world leaders that normally despised each other somehow ended up sticking up to each other. Whoever this concerns, you know yourselves.

Hypocrisy, after all, is the motor of politics as we understand it today. Mr. Navron perfectly said it when he described the disconnect between the personal relationships of world leaders and the national ties of their respective countries. The general public beyond this political compound and across the world cannot understand these personal relationships - all they hear about are sensationalized news stories about global tensions. Look closer and you will find a trade war discussed over Peanut Butter and Nutella, North-South conspiracies framed through World Cups and East-West divides bridged by a simple Bridge of Nations that all of you, sometimes with shots of Stolichnaya, have travelled through.

The Syrian refugee crisis, too, was subject to this personalization process - there you were, inside this compound, discussing how to effectively split this homeless population as though you were splitting a bag of peanuts. It is perhaps telling that Mr. Saito died from a single peanut - in essence, what he choked on were Syrian refugees, a banished single people that a powerful group as yourselves could not even agree on splitting, cutting and shredding into fifteen bites.

Who killed Mr. Saito already?

The first person I will charge with his murder is the Canadian Prime Minister. *I must be mistaken?* German Chancellor, calm down. Enough with the laughter, Mr. Chump. Mr. Judeaux, after much deliberation, I do not believe that your politeness and Canadian niceness is sufficient vindication. You have been instrumental in making sure Mr. Saito takes his poison. Not only were you the vehicle that transported the PeanuTart bar from Nejmeh Square to the British Suite, but you were also the person who kept the Japanese President's emergency syringe away from him when you wore his blazer jacket and took off to help the German Chancellor with her odd obsession with recycling.

This brings me to you, Ms. Angels. You are the second person I charge this murder with. *No, Ms. Yosef, you didn't know it all along.* Ms. Angels, your engineering skills were the brains stringing this murder plot together. Your refurbishing of the whole compound as though it was a German recycling center disrupted the whole meeting. If it weren't for you and your countless orders for the sake of Mother Nature, not only would the Canadian Prime Minister not have fitted so unnoticeably in your ecological plans, but the British PM, *the third person I charge*, would not have been justified in keeping the air-conditioner of her suite on low to please you and Mr. Judeaux.

This drastic change of temperature completely tired an already-exhausted Mr. Saito, who had to remove his blazer because of the heat and could not even recognize it afterward - let alone recognize that the chocolate bar he was eating was not some left-over in his own blazer but the PeanuTart bar brought into this compound by both Mr. Chump and Mr. Navron.

You two are also complicit in the plot. *No, Mr. Chump, you cannot pardon yourself.* After much mystery about where this PeanuTart bar came from, and since it would have been too easy to point fingers at Ms. Therese's own stacks of PeanuTart bars after her debacle in our agriculture session, the poison Mr. Saito inhaled originated from outside the compound, in the special convenience store that Mr. Chump and Mr. Navron visited under the pretext of some rivalry over Peanut

Butter and Nutella. This weapon of the crime was perfectly placed in the recyclables-only bin in Nejmeh Square, the checkpoint spot that can be inconspicuously visited by ecological freaks like Ms. Angels and Mr. Judeaux.

What are your motives for the crime? Good question, Ms. Angels - as usual. This is what has confused me most in this investigation - the motive, the reason that would push any one of you to release the axe on Mr. Saito. What first caught my attention was the Japanese President's decisive vote in the motion that would successfully split the refugees. *Yes, Ms. Angels, you, Mr. Judeaux, Mr. Navron and Ms. Therese all voted for this motion.* Good observation, which would normally make Mr. Chump the sole culprit in this case.

This was what I was going for at first. I had placed most of my attention on the leaders that voted against the motion, such as Mr. Wei and Mr. Yutin, who had scheduled a behind-the-doors meeting with Mr. Saito that supposedly attempted to shatter the deal we were reaching over splitting refugees.

And you are right, Ms. Angels - these two are also charged with the murder. *Don't you take another step forward, Mr. Yutin.* Both of you were the two delegates that stood the closest to the British Suite, and it is no coincidence that your congregating at the door of the Japanese Suite in fact built the necessary obstacle for a poor, limping and old Mr. Saito. Had he not stumbled and tripped against both of your bodies in a case so filled with timed accuracies, he would have reached his suite, used his emergency syringe, and still be present with us today. *But Mr. Saito was late?*

He was not, Mr. Yutin. Your Muslim accomplices - the Saudi king, the Turkish President, and the Iranian President - whom I also hereby charge with the murder, made sure that Mr. Saito would have his poison at the very time you two congregated in front of the British Suite. This backdrop of Sunni-Shiite tensions was perfect to move the plot forward. Mr. Ourani's self-praising of his own fasting got the sympathetic Japanese President to fast in solidarity with him - and he would have definitely been alive today had the Affair of the Plastic Cups involved and energized him, instead of Mr. Al Oud. But having Mr. Saito break his fast on the Shiite time was risky - he would have easily rushed past the West Hallway, entered his room, and injected himself with the emergency syringe inside.

The Sunni-Shiite tensions in this meeting, so insistently revived by Mr. Al Oud, formed the perfect backdrop for the Turkish President to tamper with the watch he offered to Mr. Saito to thank him for fasting in solidarity with Muslims. The clock was fifteen minutes behind - accurately, so as to have Mr. Saito rush into the West Hallway at this specific time, which, by then, would be blocked by the toned bodies of Mr. Wei and Mr. Yutin. If it weren't for this clock change, I am positive, Mr. Saito would have reached his emergency syringe.

What about the stack of syringes with his designated security guard? Perfect observation, Mr. Andoghram, but your question will not be able to pluck holes into my conclusions. You are right in that the emergency syringes with this private bodyguard could have saved the life of Mr. Saito. But the inaccessibility of this security detail should be credited to the sneaky women of this meeting - Ms. Yosef, Ms. Maseko, Ms. David and of course, the all-innocent Ms. Springborg. *Let me finish, Ms. Yosef.*

All four of you, it has appeared to me, were instrumental in depriving Mr. Saito from his rescue boat, his special bodyguard's additional stacks of syringes. The backdrop here was not religious rivalry but gender. During the hour leading up to 7:45PM, all of you were at the Swedish Suite, where you supposedly talked about how gross Mr. Chump is - a *fitting* recurrent theme throughout the last three days. This was perfect to justify the ensuing uproar in the Bridge of Nations that led not only to a big bust-up between Ms. Yosef and Mr. Chump but also involved the famed slap of Ms. Springborg. By that point, Ms. David had already ushered Mr. Saito's bodyguard into the Bridge of Nations to stop the fight and this is how the last of the emergency syringes ended up completely inaccessible to and remote from Mr. Saito.

My verdict is therefore the following: I charge *each and every single one of you* for the murder of the Japanese President, Mr. Saito. This is why I could not fit the puzzle pieces together. Because you were all in on it. Each one of you contributed to one engine of this crime machine, in a way that would seem unnoticeable given your known cultural habits - be it recycling, sectarian intolerance, feminism, or whatever other ploy you used to veil your true intentions.

Of course, I wondered why you all opted to plan this murder rather than simply vote unanimously against the motion. Well, this is how we are brought back to this idea of hypocrisy, so wonderfully put by Mr. Chump himself in the very beginning of my interviews. The American, in his love to foolishly praise himself, criticized the hypocrisy of liberal nations such as Canada, Germany, Britain and France - doubting their repetitive pledges to the general public for the rights of refugees.

This perfectly illustrates the world we have come to live in today: a polar world, of good versus evil, liberal versus conservative, left-wing versus right-wing, us versus them. *A false binary*, of course, because none of you really cares about the lives of Syrian refugees. The infernal machine of the world is in motion and always must be in motion: liberals must be asking for progress; conservatives must be denying it. As a result, progress is always slow and mediocre, and often delayed until the rope must be gradually released by the conservatives.

In this case, the liberal, loving world leaders as yourselves, Ms. Angels and co, could not leave this meeting without remaining true to your initial promises to the public. You had to maintain the status-quo, the us versus them narrative that shapes the 21st century and which ordinary people, beyond this compound, are so accustomed to. The media could not, at the end of a failed meeting, denounce all of you as refugee-hating leaders.

Who is the hero of our world, after all? It wouldn't make sense to the general public, to the Game of Thrones series they are watching on the news channel - a series that must have good and evil characters, and an entertaining, and most of all *binge-worthy long* battle between them. Hence, a sudden complication had to arise. It couldn't be that the good characters had just suddenly decided to be evil too. The sudden death of one of the delegates was your Deus Ex Machina - Mr. Saito was 80 years old anyway, and you can blame it on peanuts.

What should I do, then? Normally, I should listen to the first advice I received from the American President. *Lock everyone up.*

BREAKING NEWS:

Amid Tragedy, World Leaders Reportedly Reach Historical Humanitarian Deal

I can hear you perfectly, Cheryl. I'm reporting to you live from Nejmeh Square in downtown Beirut. You can see next to me countless news reporters and their respective team and crew reporting from all around the world to witness this historical event in a city all-too-familiar with history's unexpected moments of turbulence. The chaos, in this case, was the confirmed suicide of the Japanese President, who had left a note that the Lebanese authorities have shared with us earlier.

As a reminder for our viewers, the 80-year-old Japanese President has taken his own life as a sacrifice to the pains of Syrians and as a warning to a divided international community that, up until then, had yet been moved enough to find a pressing solution to a growing and uncared for refugee population here in Lebanon. What we are now hearing from Nejmeh Square is that a deal has apparently been reached for the fate of these refugees. World leaders have only just started leaving the conference room after a swooping six consecutive hours inside. This dedication is clearly a direct result of the Japanese President's suicide, which reportedly left all the heads of nations in a state of complete dismay, confusion and horror.

We see the American President approaching the square. President Chump, has a deal been indeed reached and what are its outcomes?

RONALD CHUMP: A huge deal, buddy, a huge deal. We have mutually decided, upon much pressure from the American delegation, to proportionally, rather than equally, distribute the Syrian population here in Lebanon among the participating fifteen nations. Needless to say that America remains the biggest economy in the whole world, which means that we will be championing the biggest number of refugees in due time. China, of course, is up next with the second biggest responsibility - their infrastructure is of course less ready than America's, so it will be interesting to see how they manage that. Regardless, the world should be very much indebted to the way the American delegation has handled this meeting - since World War I we haven't showed this much selfless devotion for humanity.

You have just heard the American President's statement live from Nejmeh Square. Now confirmed, there had been indeed talks about the nations opting for a proportional division of the Syrian population rather than an equal one. The latter option was reportedly dropped after rejections from nations with less stable economies, such as Brazil. There she is, Ms. Vilma Yosef, smiling gladly at her American counterpart as they shake hands. There is also the Iranian President caught in a warm embrace with his Russian counterpart. Right next to them we see emerging the

German Chancellor, who remains stern-faced despite the diplomatic victory. Chancellor Angels, are you satisfied with the deal Germany has reached with its fellow nations?

MARKELLA ANGELS: Of course, I am very satisfied. The German delegation has tried its best to push for a deal that is feasible and effective to all but that also upholds the values we hope to spread in this time of internationalization. One provision to the deal, for example, is Germany's pledge of three million dollars to the Lebanese government to boost its recycling system, which has been paralyzed since the overwhelming arrival of Syrian refugees. The American delegation has also pledged to return to the Paris Treaty, another ecological step to make sure our helping of refugees for a better future parallels our work to preserve any future at all on this Earth.

Thank you very much, her excellency. You have just heard from the German Chancellor, who detailed to us some of the provisions attached to this sweeping deal. The British Prime Minister is now also seen stepping out of the political compound. Prime Minister Therese, did the United Kingdom reach the deal they had envisioned prior to coming to Beirut?

MAYA THERESE: Absolutely, absolutely. From the very start, the British delegation has strived to promote the idea that welcoming these refugees does not have to be an economic burden to participating countries. Provisions to the Accord include new trade deals with the United Kingdom, such as trades with America's peanut industry as well as mutually-remunerative deals with Lebanon's soap industry. Of course, as you know with *Brexit*, the necessity of innovating *post-Brexit deals* has become crucial to the *post-Brexit era* in world trade. This deal is indeed historical, surely to be remembered in the long-term to be as remarkable as *Brexit* itself.

This was the British Prime Minsiter live from Beirut. This is all we have at the moment, Cheryl, as the world leaders seem to gear up for a minute of silence at the square in memory of the late Japanese President. This humanitarian breakthrough surely would never have materialized if it weren't for a martyr like President Saito, who shook the international community in his wake. The world leaders have now lined up. They certainly look extremely proud of themselves. And in a world that up until yesterday looked gloomily decisive, perhaps they rightfully should be.

THE TRUTH ACCORDING

TO REFUGEE YASMEEN DAWOOD

When did your parents leave Syria, Mr. Fakhouri? In the early 70s, I see. They fled from one unstable country to another, as Lebanon geared up then to enter its own destructive civil war. That's when my own family left Lebanon, both the Lebanese and Syrian sides, to Australia. I was born there and by that time my parents had adjusted somewhat rapidly. There had been already a significant Lebanese diaspora in Melbourne, and they gave them the right directions to settle in.

The most important piece of advice was to change their names. Dawood was too weird to the Australian tongue - *David* was better, and it was anyway the family name's literal English translation. That's why my parents chose the name Jasmine for me - it was equal to Yasmeen, its Arabic origin.

I'm assuming you must have a lot of Lebanese roots, given your ability to be named as Prime Minister in a country, which, since the Syrian War, has seen a rise of xenophobia against its Syrian population. But I guess roots can be easily covered. Look at me, Prime Minister of Australia. I look no different than an Ashley next door or a Jennifer down the block.

The mainstream media rarely mentions my roots - it was a good thing that my parents completely submerged themselves in Australian surroundings and ways. I must credit our mutual Lebanese side - oh the Lebanese, you can place him or her anywhere and they will thrive. It doesn't matter how they do so - as long as they get to where or who they want to be.

Did I talk to the other leaders? Yes, it was quite an experience. They are all still shocked and a little bit traumatized. The Swedish Prime Minister could not hold back her tears - she feels an extreme amount of guilt. Even those cruel American and Russian Presidents sounded to me extremely sympathetic... as though their egos melted away since they discovered through your marvelous speech their small individual contribution to Mr. Saito's death.

What made things worse for them is that they could not point fingers again at each other and ask who could have been the mastermind behind this plot. Because, of course, the one thing they knew for sure is that *they* didn't plot it. That's what you get when you're so cynical about everyone else: no one left to trust when you want to trust anyone at all.

I am still astounded by the way you and I pulled this off, Mr. Fakhouri. Yet, it seemed so easy to get all these world leaders to believe that they had played a part in the most intricate political assassination known to history. After all, we really didn't have to do much, you and I. They themselves played their cards exactly as we knew they would. Let's rewind and see how exactly these so-called leaders played as pawns in our own game for humanity.

The timeline starts with the PeanuTart bar that Mr. Chump and Mr. Navron got from the special convenience store in Nejmeh Square. Especially for them, indeed. Of course, I had to kick-start things when I evoked America's love for peanut butter in that agriculture-focused session. This, as we calculated, would be the source of a long elegy from Mr. Chump about peanut butter and placing him next to the French President was a great way to get the debate over the primacy between PeanuTart and Nutella started. It was also smart to place the German Chancellor next to them and predict that the talkative and rude American President would continue the chat on written notes.

Besides that, we knew from the start that the French President would go along with Mr. Chump's mindless talk because of the threatened trade war at stake. The last step was to make sure there was no trash can in the whole of Nejmeh Square except for the famed recyclables-only bin. We should thank the American President himself for complaining that climate change was a Chinese hoax - a guarantee of the right attitude. I believe one of your agents anyway still went to check whether that unsealed PeanuTart bar was perfectly, and recklessly, tossed in the recyclables-only bin.

Then came our helpful Canadian, driving a highly-demanding Mercedes Benz, Trashella. What a duo. I honestly thought we had to indirectly motivate them to step up their recycling duties. It was simply enough to have the event coordinators place one single recyclables-only bin in the whole wide radius to get that Mercedes running fast and furious across the hallways. Thanks to her organized regimen, Mr. Judeaux was able to pick up our poison and transport it all the way to the British Suite.

Oh the British Suite. Everything happened smoothly there. 1) Have the two overly-polite people, the Canadian and Japanese leaders, show up by themselves. 2) Have the British woman sink the room into a sauna to please Germany and Canada then see her take her guests to Alaska to please Japan. 3) See an exhausted Japanese 80-year-old wear the wrong jacket and 4) get a polite Canadian to wear willingly the wrong jacket in order not to disturb the tired old man - classically Canadian, that one! I am still shocked that all of this happened organically - I was going to excuse myself from the girls at the Swedish Suite and join the British tea party to tamper with things. Fortunately, on my way to Ms. Springborg's, I saw Mr. Judeaux leave the British Suite with a blazer clearly too loose for his beauty standards.

The girls. This is my favorite bit. It was wonderful playing the role of the woman who hates feminists. The complete opposite of who I am, as you know, Mr. Fakhouri. I knew that the best way to get Ms. Yosef so enraged and worked up about Mr. Chump was to have her polar opposite constantly present with her - the more I defended men, the more she lost her temper. I opened the door, expecting Mr. Chump outside, and there you go - a Brazilian bull charging forward. *Did I expect Ms. Springborg's slap?* At all! This was the best surprise. I had already gone to usher in the security guard when things were brewing and the Swede's slap was perfect to get the guard even more concerned to stop the uproar in the Bridge of Nations.

The involvement of the Russian and Chinese Presidents was rather simple to stage. Well done on you, Mr. Fakhouri, to have tipped Russia to play a mediating role over the disputed islands between China and Japan.

The Russian's big ego and his love for Russian supremacy was enough to get him so interested in the mission. Bingo - we had two robust bodies to intercept a limping Japanese old man at the right time.

At the right exact time. This is where your genius comes into play, Mr. Fakhouri. As I am too busy with domestic Australian politics, I have been rather disconnected about the sectarian tensions between Sunnis and Shiites recently. I didn't even know that Iran had pressured its religious authorities to have the time to break one's fast to be fifteen minutes before Sunnis. It always used to be the Sunnis who ate first - but then again, both have been racing for a while now over who represents true Islam, and it is not uncommon to see weird religious decisions being used as political devices.

The device we needed, of course, was Mr. Andoghram's watch. Your Sunnis-only meeting with the Saudi and Turkish heads of states was anyway doomed to be about fighting off the Iranian specter in the region, since Mr. Al Oud kept bringing this up by himself. I wonder how you pulled off keeping the conversation deep and hateful enough to get Mr. Andoghram to later decide to tamper with the watch. He must have felt, after that meeting, that he had a duty to protect his Sunni brothers from Iran.

I can't blame Mr. Saito to have proposed to fast along; the respectful Japanese President, after all, was the only person who didn't alienate Mr. Ourani during this meeting because of Iran's presence in Syria. He told me before breakfast how sorry he felt for him - and this is where I made him feel so bad about poor Mr. Ourani, enough to propose a crazy idea to make him feel better. The true price of kindness, right there. The fasting was perhaps as fatal to an exhausted Mr. Saito as the peanuts themselves. Ramadan Kareem, I suppose!

Cheers, Mr. Fakhouri. This *double* cover-up would not have been possible without you. Everyone won, after all. You got the Syrian refugees to move to relatively more habitable and peaceful countries, before Lebanon's xenophobia drove them back to the Syrian War.

I never told you my own motive? Well, Mr. Fakhouri, I will confess that my motivation was a little *unLebanese* of me, that is it had nothing to do with something I could tangibly gain. I proposed to you this plan a few months ago because I had grown tired of my short time in office. I am so glad I can now resign and blame it on some populist party bitching about the Syrians I'm bringing back to Australia with me. Politics, after all, is not for me.

This frustration came from the inaction we have witnessed toward Syria; a country I hold more dearly than Lebanon only because its tragedy is not brought with its own hands. This UN meeting was a perfect testament to this inaction - for the most part, we talked about everything and anything in the world but Syrian refugees. Politicians are more preoccupied with diplomatic wars, conspiracies and statistics than real, human lives.

Seeing this political irresponsibility, so perfectly ignored by the general public and the infotainment media they are exposed to, I could not remain in office, the place from which I thought I could exercise change. Politics today is no longer the answer for political change - at least not in the way we now conceive politics to look like. *How does it look like?* One suffices to observe the recent events of Nejmeh Square, which hosted, instead of a UN meeting, a global party of elite leaders travelling to and fro, hand in hand, across the Bridge of Nations, drinking vodka and giggling over stupid Chump jokes and football.

You see, Mr. Fakhouri, it quite terrifies me, the world we have come to live in. A world never so connected, yet never so isolating. America First, Britain First, Russia First, China First, and so on. Look at yourself, Mr. Fakhouri, you are the head of the Lebanese government, and though you have Syrian blood, your own party ran on the rhetoric of Lebanon First, which meant Syria Second.

It is this selfish nationalism that truly pushed me to devise such a plan - from which, regrettably, an old man had to be spared. But do human lives mean anything anymore? Stalin might have been right when he said that one death is a tragedy, a million... a statistic. A Japanese President dies and he is a martyr. Millions of lives in Syria have been tarnished since 2011 and they are mere numbers, pictures to rush past on our social timelines, voices to mute on our televisions.

I wanted these world leaders, who are responsible to these deaths from their mere accepting of leading a nation in a globalized world, to see their mistake. To understand what it feels like to actually kill someone. This was my true motivation, Mr. Fakhouri. Because these world leaders already have blood on their hands, Syrian blood. But unfortunately, it is invisible, as invisible as your refugees.

But now, they will live the rest of their lives wondering what this mess at Nejmeh Square was all about. Asking themselves at their loneliest moment at night whether they should feel bad that they had inadvertently caused the death of an innocent old man. Wondering forever whether they were truly responsible for blood that matters a lot more to some distant family or nation than their own.

Isn't the world's inaction toward the Syrian War rooted in this disconnect? That the lives of distant strangers mean less than those up close. Ironically enough, these world leaders would have been spared from this murder if they all thought, spoke and acted as human beings, rather than as German, American, Canadian and so on. What you and I did was merely exploit their national and cultural habits, which, at this point, are extremely predictable. They did the rest.

If the German Chancellor cared less about Germany's environmental policies, if the American President cared less about American Peanut Butter - gosh, if the Canadian PM cared less about *Canadian niceness*, all these leaders would have spared themselves from thrusting forward, blindly, in an infernal machine of clashing cultures, one that produces crimes without criminals and victims without burials.

In some way, these leaders would have been spared this murder had they been more *human*. Humanity... this is the last stage; the last utopia we are still aspiring to reach. Because Mr. Fakhouri, we fool ourselves every single time we use that word, *human*. We talk about human casualties. We study human societies. We deal with humanitarian crises. It has become a cheap word we toss around without ever seeing our own reflection in it.

We are not human yet, Mr. Fakhouri. We really aren't. It is still not in our consciousness, not yet a result of our evolutionary mechanism. We still think of ourselves as part of a tribe. As American. As Russian. And from there we draw boundaries and we include some and exclude others. Can't one be both Lebanese and Syrian, like you and I? That's too complicated for the Game of Thrones series people are watching. Outliers have no business in entertainment. Keep the script simple, and the characters even simpler.

Do I regret what we did? Less than I thought, to tell you the truth. After all, I did no different than those world leaders, Mr. Fakhouri. How can I regret staying true to my closest roots, *Lebanese*? We don't recycle and we don't love peanut butter. We make business.

You know it best... the Lebanese mind is business-oriented, a problem-solver... perhaps because of the many political instabilities our people have had to adapt to. That's all I did. I made business like a Lebanese. I negotiated like a Lebanese. A Lebanese seller, after all, always makes sure to be on the more profitable end of any transaction. My biggest crime is that indeed. Selling. Selling Syrians, *Lebanese style*.

THE END

ABOUT THE AUTHOR

Rayyan Dabbous is a young Lebanese writer with Syrian roots. His previous book, *Bad Men*, was published by Arab Scientific Publishers when he was 17. It wasn't that good.

He is also a playwright (*Up For Grabs America*) and filmmaker (*In Search of the Last Agora*). His articles have featured in The Daily Star, Open Democracy, Global Research, Open Global Rights, and others. His more genuine writings can be found on his Instagram.

He is the founder of Boumerang Foundation. Nothing fancy. Feel free to contact him via boumerang.org

www.ingramcontent.com/pod-product-compliance
Lightning Source LLC
Chambersburg PA
CBHW020616130626
46552CB00013B/1923